SO LOVELY TO KILL

HARRISON WADE

WILDSIDE PRESS

A GRAPHIC ORIGINAL

Cover by Barye Phillips

PART ONE

Out of the Pan . . .

1

SHE WAS as warm and bouncy and pretty as any gal, that Agnes. Her lips were pure flame, her hair a glittering ebony, and when I retreated from the sticky heat of the morning and entered her air-conditioned office, saw her sitting bright and pert in a white nylon uniform, I got that itchy feeling all over again.

I bent down and pecked her on the cheek and she purred. Her mouth fell open, exhibiting a deep, dark hunger for love or passion or both. "John Fury!" she teased. "Private eye, public droop." Her voice had all the innocence of a mating call.

"How's my baby?" I said, and this time gave her a buzz smack on those round, red lips.

"Business is dead," she said—a shop joke—and she rested her hand on the side of my face. I drew back automatically and felt a shiver ice through my body. I hunched my shoulders as the uneasiness took hold and, suddenly, I was unhappy about the whole thing.

Agnes frowned. "Not still?" she said sadly.

"Sorry, baby, I didn't think it showed."

Of course it showed and I could have walloped myself for it, but that's the way it was. Her lips I could take and they could have bruised me until my skin turned blue. Not the hands. Once they got inquisitive, I chilled fast and desire was snuffed like water on flame.

It had been that way from our very first date. Her vibrating body, her soft, husky voice and her exciting laugh kept me wanting her. The hands drove me away. And I guess that's the way it will always be. Unless . . .

Oh, what's the use. I just can't take it. Imagine! Your woman, the superintendent of the city morgue!

"You should go into some genteel profession," I said defensively.

"Like what?"

"Like bull-fighting or lady-wrestling or maybe you could drive a garbage truck."

She stood and thrust those two sharp orbs of loveliness against my chest and her arms encircled my waist. "You'll get used to it, Johnny." The way she said it made me quake.

I said mockingly, "How many cadavers have you fondled this morning?"

"Not one, so there's nothing to worry about." She stroked my face again. For the second time I froze, faked relaxation and tried to admit with my eyes that it wasn't so horrible after all.

"Is the lieutenant here yet?" I asked.

"He's in the deep freeze, so you'd better hurry. You're rather late, you know."

I quaked again. That damned deep freeze. It was an extremely plain room, properly chilled, and the element that made it ghastly was the double row of vaults set in three of the four walls. Then there was the incongruity of knowing that Lieutenant Matt Nugent was down there waiting for me. He was a strange cop—a crazy one. Long ago I learned that lobsters can be classified as: (A) cynical; (B) grouchy; (C) both. He was the paradox.

He was jolly. A guy gets sieved with the slightly un-

SO LOVELY TO KILL

dainty pellets of a .38 and everyone weeps. Not Matt
Nugent. "The man's dead. Ho-ho! Hilarious, huh?" It
wasn't that he was morbid exactly. He just liked to laugh.
And I knew that his big blue eyes would be shining like
Irish emeralds, his fleshy, pink face quivering with joy.
Happiness in the morgue. It gave me the creeps.

"What does he want with me?" I asked, because the
early morning telephone call had explained nothing.

She chuckled and took two deep breaths. Two of those
were quite a sight to see. "He wants to scare your pants
off and then do a fast tattoo."

"Huh?"

"That's right," she intoned, suggesting that it was and
was not a great big joke.

She wiggled over to the basement door, opened it and
extended a left-handed invitation. "Come on. Follow
bouncy little me."

I followed, wishing I didn't have to.

Matt had rested his hulk on the edge of a desk and,
since he wore only a faint smile, I knew he was thinking
real deep. They must have been pleasant thoughts, like
barking a Thompson submachine gun at a crowd of pedestrians, because it took a greeting to woo him out of his
daydream.

Then he laughed, "Johnny, my boy," and this was ac-
cented by a few more robust ho-ho's. "Am I glad to see
you. Yes, sir, real glad." He grabbed my hand and began
to pump for oil and I wondered what the pitch was. I had
seen him only yesterday and he had told me to go to
hell. "You sure gave us a scare last night. You sure did."

"Last night?" I said. "Last night I was home in bed."

"Sure you were. Sure. I'm damned glad you were."

I shrugged. Even cops go crazy. Then again, the deep
freeze might have had something to do with it. It was

9

gray and dismal, voices echoed like volcanic rumblings and the air was stale, reluctant to enter the lungs. It was a place where sane remarks could sound stupid.

I waited for Matt to go on. He didn't. He just stood there, grinning at me, a jubilant father who had found the prodigal son. I felt embarrassed. Also suspicious.

"What do you want me to do, kill somebody?"

This was the funniest thing he had ever heard and his closed fist thumped on my arm. In an hour there would be a bruise and I would carry it for a week.

"A job, John. A job."

"For money?"

"For thirty thousand bucks!"

I looked at him quizzically. "Yeah?"

He said earnestly, "I mean it."

I was frowning now. "Thirty thousand in real United States money? You're offering me a job for that?"

He nodded and I whistled and didn't even mind when it screamed around the room, sounding like the cry of a prehistoric bird. Thirty thousand! This was music, a thousand violins. Thirty thousand violins! And did I need it. Hell, I needed ten bucks. Not that I was limping along at the ragged edge of the financial world, but I was expanding and when you start to pay a new detective $5,000 per, in addition to two others who pull better salaries, you need that green stuff, but bad.

There was a gimmick, of course. There had to be. No private eye gets that kind of dough for a job. In fact, most of my cohorts in the racket are lucky if they don't starve to death. Joe Lance, believe it or not, has to make book on the side, and he's a darned god detective.

I was real skeptical now. "All right, Nugent, what gives?"

He turned his back to me without replying, and we

both watched Agnes leaf through her register. It was a simple affair that recorded arrivals and departures, and in a matter of seconds she found what she was looking for.

She said, much too gaily, "He's in Number Ten. Do you want to see him now?"

Matt nodded. "And then we do a fast tattoo."

There was that talk again. But I was protesting against something else. "Look, I don't have to look at a corpse, do I?"

"Good God!" said Matt. "What a weak-livered detective you are."

"Well," I defended. "I just don't like them."

"This one you might like." His tone was less ebullient now.

"Sure," said Agnes. "This one is pretty. You won't be able to tear yourself away."

The mirth had left her voice, too, and her lips were pressed thin. She went to Crypt Number Ten, twisted the chrome handle and pulled out the slab, as though she did it every day—as she did. Her actions were accompanied by a cloudburst of cold, condensing air. There was a body there, of course, but I did not look at it. Sobered, and feeling lousy about the whole thing, I turned to Matt.

"An identification?" I said.

"Come on," he said and took me by the arm. "Just don't pass out or nothing like that."

"What's he got, three eyes?"

I was trying to bolster my courage. I didn't bolster it enough. Maybe that's why Matt didn't answer me. Maybe he couldn't talk either. I know I couldn't and my wiseacre attitude was whisked away like a feather in a gale. I did a double take and froze. The feather was blown back again and it took refuge in my stomach. There it fluttered and flapped and made my knees bend. Matt's hand was on

11

my arm. It was not needed, but it felt good, just the same. Agnes' face was pinched and she studied my reaction pensively, not looking at the corpse.

"You all right?" said Matt.

The air hissed out of my lungs and, feeling hollow inside, I quickly sucked it back in again. "Christ, you should warn a guy!"

He said nothing. Just stood there.

"Well!" I was angry now.

He shrugged. "I wanted to make it impressive."

"You sure as hell succeeded!" I bounced on him with a few more choice adjectives and appropriate nouns.

I looked back at the body. The guy who once owned it was young, about thirty, and he wasn't bad looking, with azure eyes, a strong, straight nose and thin lips that had, during the final, eternal moment, twisted themselves into a crooked, mocking smile. His hair was a light blonde, his brows bushy. His muscles were long and lithe, like a baseball player's. He was tall, maybe six one and weighed maybe one-eighty-five.

I didn't know him.

I had never seen him before.

But this didn't make the sight of him any the less brutal. I had been stunned, cruelly, and my momentary reflex of anger probably saved me from babbling.

Somewhere around me came that stupid talk again. Matt was asking if the tattoo man had arrived and Agnes was saying he had. The words were wee fragments, waltzing close to my consciousness, yet not quite strong enough to reach the core.

The guy on the slab. I just couldn't get over it. Had I not been standing there, alive, breathing, I would have sworn that I was looking at me!

12

2

MATT NUGENT told Agnes to beat it and she did, after first redepositing the body in the vault. We went back to the desk. Matt rested his ample posterior on the top and crossed his thick legs. I fell into the chair. I was drained, enervated. I was sure my normal ruddy complexion was a sickly white.

The jolly lobster said nothing and gave me time to reassemble the scattered pieces of my brain. Coherence didn't return quickly. The shock had been too great, too sudden. It was distasteful enough to forego breakfast and hightail it to the city's haberdashery for human has-beens. To be exposed as a corpse myself was vulgar.

Of course, upon reflection, I knew it couldn't have been me. There were differences, several. The guy's hair was blonde; mine a sort of red. The guy's ears flapped out a little too far and had lobes that hung like balls; my ears were small and close to my head. He didn't have a mustache. I did, though it's so thin it's hardly discernible. But when a thing like that happens you don't think about differences—take it all in all, I'd seen a preview of Johnny Fury.

I gulped huge quantities of the putrid air, attempting to satisfy my lungs' hunger, and began to understand small things that were of minor significance. I knew now why

13

Agnes' lips had responded so lovingly. I knew why Matt had jostled me with such uncoplike affection. I wasn't dead. They were glad. They were friends. Someone else was dead—virtually a twin, and it was a miracle of coincidence.

I said evenly, forcing my conviction through clamped teeth, "You son of a plowhorse—what a way to start my day!"

He laughed. It was a liquid, gurgling spray and his fat, cherubic face beamed like a middle-aged kewpie doll. "What are you kicking about? You're here, aren't you?" Indicating that I wasn't on the slab.

"Yeah, I'm here. God!"

I withdrew a pack of butts, flipped one to Matt and, rudely ignoring the no-smoking sign, we rolled two columns of blue-gray up to the ceiling.

"Feeling better?" he asked.

"Sure, like a million. Great. Just great." I sucked on the weed, billowed out a cloud, sucked again. "Who is he? My long lost brother?"

He shrugged. "About that I wouldn't know."

"What do you know?"

That imbecilic grin again. "Plenty, and none of it is particularly good."

"For instance?"

"Well, his name is Charles Apple Renney. Apple is a nickname. He was thirty-one. At the age of sixteen he held up a finance company, was convicted and given a suspended sentence. He was tried twice for bank robbery and acquitted each time.

"Him?" I said sadly. "That nice, clean-cut chap?"

Matt snarled, "He's clean-cut like a bellhop in a cathouse. Before his sudden departure from this fickle vale—"

"Cut the theatrics."

"—of tears, he was working himself up high in the

14

SO LOVELY TO KILL

California syndicate—numbers, horses, slot machines, the works. Oh, yes! He was once pulled in on a murder rap, but there wasn't enough evidence to bring him to trial."

Of course he was kidding. A specimen so purely virile, so obviously American couldn't possibly have been connected with those naughty pastimes. Other people did those things. He just held their coats.

I said, "What else do you know?"

The lecture continued, an incessant, instructive drone. "He owned a forty-thousand-dollar house in L.A. He was recuperating from pneumonia and that's how he died." Matt flicked ashes on the cold tile floor and shifted his prodigiousness. "Last night, late, he was running for a train and keeled over. His heart. He shouldn't have been running, the coroner says. He shouldn't have been drinking, either, which he was, heavily. He should have been flat on his back in bed."

I stood, dropped my half-finished butt on the floor, ground it dead with my sticky, gum-shoeing heel. "Well, give him a nice funeral and don't tell anyone. Maybe they won't miss him."

Matt put his hand on my chest and gently shoved me back into the chair. "Don't be so eager," he said. "There's more."

I shook my head. "I don't want to hear more. I have to go to work. There's an old lady up on Madison Avenue who wants a bodyguard for her Pekingese. A local mongrel has amorous designs."

He spread his leather lips and exposed two flawless rows of factory teeth. "What about the money?"

"What money?"

"The thirty thousand."

Oh, yes, the thirty thousand. I had forgotten about it. The moolah melody. I melted in my chair. I would do

15

a lot for thirty grand—fight a tiger with my bare hands, even eat yogurt. I nodded politely, hoping he would go on.

He didn't get the chance. Agnes popped her comely face in the room and announced blithely, "Lieutenant, the tattoo man is ready. Should I send him in?"

Matt waved her away. "No, not yet. I haven't told him."

"Told me what?" I wanted to know.

I got no response and Agnes chirped mysteriously, "Well, have him take off his trousers."

"Take off my—"

"Yes," said Matt seriously. "You'd better drop your pants." He added quietly, "And take off your shorts, too."

"My shorts—"

"You'll look awfully cute," said Agnes and she un-popped her pretty head. The sturdy door slammed.

"What the devil is this all about?" I demanded.

I was given no satisfaction. Matt fluffed me off with a shake of his meaty hand. He rose from the desk and began to walk—no place in particular, just around. Carelessly, denoting immersion in his own peculiar thoughts, his fingers fiddled with the chrome handles of the slabs. It was disgusting.

Lovingly patting the handle of Crypt Number Ten, behind which reposed the facsimile of me, he said, "Have you ever heard of Patty Sears?"

I thought about it and shook my head.

"Good," he chimed. "Then there's a good chance he never heard of you, either."

"Will you please get on with it?" I said.

"Sure, Johnny." He lumbered back to the desk, leaned forward and permitted me to swoon under the magic glow of his baby blue eyes. "Here's the deal. This Patty Sears is a local hoodlum, sort of an agent for the underworld." He saw me frown and clarified his remark. "What

16

I mean is, he's a guy who knows everybody, has a lot of contacts and, when some hood wants info on tools or anything, Patty is a good man to know. Small-time himself, he can make arrangements for a price. See?"

I nodded and he gushed on, with enthusiasm. "Well, last night when they dragged this Apple Renney down here, they thought he was you—naturally."

"Naturally."

"It wasn't until they went over his personal effects that we found out who he was. Then did the gears start to grind!"

"Like how?"

"Well, for one thing, that babe finally shut up. I had gotten here by then. God, we couldn't think straight the way she yakked."

Matt had an obnoxious habit of speaking in the abstract. He and only he knew what he was talking about. I said testily, "What babe?"

He gestured behind him. "That Agnes. She was jabbering something about a formal dinner date she had coming up with you and who the hell would take her if you were dead?"

I laughed. "That's a nice way to mourn."

Matt raised a shoulder, "Well, you know how screwy she acts sometimes, but this morning you were her passion boat again, the big man of her dreams, the one who some day would."

"Would what?"

"Would anything, just as long as it was in the same house and you both owned it jointly."

I grunted.

"Hell, I'm just a struggling private dick."

"Now," he agreed. "After this caper you might be rolling."

17

"And what about this caper," I said. "What happened next?"

"Well," Matt continued, "then the commissioner came down."

"The commissioner?" I said, surprised.

He cocked his head for emphasis. "Sure, the commissioner. This, we suddenly realize, is big stuff." He surveyed me askance, pulled a wad of papers from his inside coat pocket and thrust them upon me. "This is how big it is."

I only had to scan the papers to know what they meant. They were official and there were three copies, all duly signed with an official flourish. I had been appointed special deputy, giving me the temporary status of cop. As a lobster, temporary or not, I was given all the rights and protection that the law allowed. This was important. Even if I shot a guy, these papers, in effect, said I was "on duty."

But I still didn't get it and shrugged my shoulders. "So now I'm a cop. So what?"

"So sometimes you're not too bright, either," said Matt, arching his eyebrows. "Look, you two look alike, don't you? What we want you to do is take this Apple Renney's place."

I yawned with the boredom of it all. Like hell I did! I slid forward and perched myself on the edge of the chair, eyes wide, body rigid and ears anticipating. Propositions such as Matt had made had a twofold effect on me. First, they made my pores tingle. Second, they scared me silly.

"What do I have to do?" I asked, and sensed that my voice was squeaking at an abnormally high octave.

He replied quietly, "You'll have to team up with Manie Grass."

He might have said, "*You'll have to take on the Russian*

18

army single-handedly." I leaned back in my chair, not disturbed, only doubtful that Matt still had marbles to rattle. It was crazy.

I whispered incredulously, "You're kidding, of course."

His eyes closed and he shook his head patiently. "I'm not kidding at all."

He must have been. It made no sense. Manie Grass was a common hoodlum, one of the coarsest of the species, a throwback, in method, to the bygone era of Capone. He had been in jail so often they no longer bothered to break down his bunk. He'd return—everybody knew it. But now he was free and not wanted for a blessed thing. Oh, he was big just the same, big in size, big in reputation, a real highpockets in the criminal world. He was also lucky.

I thought back to his last escapade, more sensational than the shooting of Dillinger or the capturing of the atom spies. Manie and his cohorts, two brassy, psychopathic brothers, Tee-hee and Seymour Marchetti, had bazookaed an armored truck. That's right. Bazookaed it! On a desolate short cut between two parallel highways outside of Albany, New York, these amusing degenerates pumped one shell into the motor as the truck sped along. It was stopped cold, a twisted, shattered ogre of inanimate steel. A second shell was dumped into the hull, affording access to the money. Three men were killed, the driver and two guards, and a total of one-half million leaves of negotiable cabbage was lifted.

Only two things went wrong. From the state's standpoint—a sluggish, perhaps fear-ridden jury pronounced the Marchettis not guilty. From Manie's standpoint—the money was too hot to use. Not one bill had turned up,

19

since no fence was willing to risk handling the loot.

I shook my head in annoyance. Try as I could, I didn't understand. "You said that this Apple Renney was a comer in California?"

A nod confirmed it.

"Well, why the devil would he toss up a juicy deal like that to team up with a claw like Manie Grass?"

Matt flexed the pink fingers on his right hand and again deserted the desk. He took a position under a blue neon ceiling lamp and, at a distance of ten feet, it gave him a sickly pallor.

"Why?" he chuckled. "Why? I stopped trying to peg the criminal mind long ago. Sometimes they follow pattern, sometimes they do crazy things. All we know is that Apple Renney wanted an in with Manie Grass. We also know that he contacted Patty Sears, the agent I just told you about, and asked him to arrange it."

"Did he?"

"He did."

"How do you know this?"

"A letter we found on Renney."

"From Manie Grass?"

He nodded.

"What did it say?" I asked.

He gave me his back and I got his monotone after it caromed lifelessly off the hard walls. "It doesn't say much of anything, but it's easy to read between the lines. Our conclusion is that Manie plans to rob a bank."

Nothing was said for a long time. I just sat there and breathed. It seemed like a normal, healthy reaction.

Then I said, "And you want me to take Renney's place?"

"Uh-huh."

"And rob a bank with Manie Grass?"

20

SO LOVELY TO KILL

"Something like that," Matt said and swung around to face me.

I stood. I took in the length and breadth of his humpty-dumpty features and I was grinning my fool head off. Then I laughed. It was a deep, dyspeptic rumble.

He laughed, too, but it was a phony interlude—two grown men standing in the middle of the city morgue's deep freeze, jockeying laughter back and forth.

It ended like that. I clammed up, nodded politely and stalked swiftly from the room.

3

THEY CAUGHT me as I descended the dirty granite steps in front of the morgue, and I had been traveling fast, too. I say they caught me. They pounced on me, four rapacious eagles. Agnes tugged at my coat from behind, Matt anchored himself in front of me and leaned against my stomach, and two white-uniformed attendants, as strong and ugly as gorillas, swung from my threshing arms.

I shouted, attracting attention from gaping pedestrians, "Let me go! What do you think you're doing?"

"Shut up and come back here," said Matt, embarrassment vivid on his face. "I only want you to listen to me."

Maybe the miniature crowd that quickly gathered assumed that I was a nomadic corpse bent on escape, because they seemed to take in the wild scene with frank trepidation and there wasn't one courageous enough to come to my assistance. To me the situation reeked of low comedy. But there was nothing funny about it. It was a pie-throwing farce played so poorly that I sensed desperation. Police lieutenants don't purposely act like fools in public unless there is a reason.

Still, I didn't give in and, in a vain attempt to hold myself dignified, I fought back. In my case it was desperation. I'm a reasonable, sensible businessman. I work for money. Sometimes I have to do some smelly things. But

22

SO LOVELY TO KILL

getting involved with Manie Grass was not one of them.
Such an involvement would be feared by a criminal.
Manie liked to kill. He liked to stomp into a bank, or any
place where money was stashed, with two heavy pieces of
artillery in his hands. He liked to fire them. More often
than not his target was an innocent bystander.

So, as a reasonable, sensible businessman, I wasn't compelled to accept the authority of a special deputy, or team
up with Manie Grass. I could call my shots, and that's
what I planned to do.

But the choice at that moment wasn't mine. Bodily,
and I thought with too much ease, the quartet ushered me
back into the building, through Agnes' office, hence again
to the deep freeze. I was ranting just as obstreperously as
I could.

"If these are police methods, Nugent, you can shove
them—"

"Tuttut," said Agnes hastily, "there's a lady present."

"You!" I roared. "A lady! A creepy morgue keeper!"

She became again, suddenly, the hard woman with the
cold hands, but she graced me with a triumphant smile
and bounced from the room. I didn't bother to appreciate
the wiggle of her ways. Somewhere a telephone was
ringing.

Then there was silence and I was guarded as though
I were an ax killer, by Matt and the one attendant. The
other had departed with Agnes, but soon he returned,
rolling in front of him one of those sinister meat wagons.
I had seen them in hospitals, a sensible means of transpor-
tation for non-ambulatory patients. I had the crawling
feeling that here not one "patient" had ever been aware
of his ride.

So there were three of them again, Matt and those two
mountains of muscle, glaring at me. Their expressions

belied truth. All I could see was frame and it was inscribed indelibly on their pasty faces.

Matt said quietly, "Johnny, you know what it means to
the department to get Manie Grass."

"Sure," I said. "Sure, I know. I rob a bank and become public hero number one, a super-duper star witness
for the state. Crabs! I become the target for every trigger-
happy hood in town." I shoved one of the attendants
away from me and glared at Matt. "Uh-uh, not Manie
Grass. You don't get to him by using tricks. His type you
shoot between the eyes."

"Manie Grass is only part of it," insisted Matt. "What
the devil, I'm not trying to execute you. I'm trying to do
a job and only you can do it for me." He waved his arm
toward Crypt Number Ten. "There's the answer in there.
How many times in a lifetime does this happen?"

I smiled faintly. "Never, as far as I'm concerned. Now,
if you'll only get out of my way—"

He was not in a generous frame of mind. He nodded,
more like a gang leader than a rational cop, and the two
mastodons moved in on me. They gripped my arms,
holding me helpless, and dragged me on top of the meat
wagon, stomach down. My musty complaint of "police
methods" now smacked home. In his awkward, bullying
way Matt was giving substance to my philosophy that
lobsters are little different from criminals. Give a criminal
a gun and he's a king. Give a cop a gun and he wears the
same crown. But add the authority of a badge and you
sometimes get a dictator. I liked Matt. I trusted him.
It felt like a hot poker to lose respect for him, too, and
that was what was happening.

I struggled feebly and Matt, not pausing, lectured to
me calmly. "All right. So you won't do it. You say that
now. But I think you're going to and, in the meantime,

we can't waste time. Time! That's what this is all about. We have things to do. You're due in an upstate resort town called Ogsinto tonight. You're to go to a farmhouse run by a man named Causby. That's where Manie and his family are staying and somewhere around there they're going to pull a bank job." He plopped his amber face three inches from mine. "So until you finally say no give me a break, will you?"

"Go to hell."

His shoulders sagged, he sighed and his face recaptured some of that phony joviality. "Okay, boys, hold him tight. I guess we have to do it the hard way."

They held me tight, all right, puncturing a few million blood vessels, and Matt acted so quickly I scarcely had an opportunity to complain. Reaching under me, he unbuckled my belt and, *swish,* like that, he yanked off my trousers and shorts. I was half nude and I'll be damned if I didn't feel like half a man.

"Give me back my pants!" I roared, and my eruption was deeper than a consumptive fog horn. "I'll see the D.A. about this."

Perhaps I would see the D.A. some time, but not then, because, with an unmasculine prance, the one attendant romped from the deep freeze, carrying my modesty with him.

I climbed off the wagon and faced Matt. I was seething and my face was probably flushed the same color as my hair. "Nugent, just who the hell do you think you are?"

He said quietly, "You'd better climb back on that thing. Agnes might come in."

Agnes wasn't on my mind. I advanced toward him, my knuckles tight and pure alabaster, and I was all set to swing when it happened. He was right, the lucky son of Erin, because the door swung open and the brazen hussy slipped into the room. Concurrently, I dove for the meat wagon. I didn't quite make it in time and the attendant quickly broke open a sheet and scaled it over me.

I know darn well she caught a glimpse of flying me, because her head dropped demurely and her face colored. But she was a babe with plenty of poise and she didn't bat one of her two long eyelashes.

As though I were buried under a thousand pelts of ermine, she muttered evenly, "It was your office telephoning, Lieutenant Nugent. They picked up Patty Sears and booked him in the midtown station."

"What charge?"

"They said they haven't thought of one yet, but they'll pick a good one. He'll be held all day."

"Good," elated Matt. "Excellent."

He came back to me, bending so close I could feel his breath. "See, Johnny? This afternoon you'll go to the tombs and see Patty. He knew Apple Renney personally and if you can bluff your way past him, you can bluff your way past anyone."

I was so perturbed I could hardly keep the facts straight. Somewhere off on a flimsy cloud was the recollection that Patty Sears was the underworld's agent—the cobra who arranged things.

At that moment, however, I had a one-track mind. I said coldly, "Get me those pants. Then, maybe, we can talk. Not before."

Agnes seemed to be enjoying my discomfort and her voice was thick with mirth. "Don't be such a prude. I've seen nude men before."

"Sure you have. Dead ones."

She faked a sigh. "You can't have everything." She bent down and planted a dainty kiss on my cheek. "Some day you won't be prudish with me—ever!"

26

SO LOVELY TO KILL

I knew what she had in mind—the matter of little feet, legalized by a tiny, gold band. I shied away from a commitment and wallowed in silence.

Matt shook his head, indicating that this wasn't the time for idle chatter. "Beat it," he said to her, "and tell that tattoo guy to get down here."

There was that insane talk again and I buried my face in the stingy softness of the meat wagon. I heard Matt move toward me and I felt his hand rest on the small of my back. "You ready to listen now?"

"I'm ready to listen," I said sarcastically. "I have one big choice, don't I?"

"You'll make your own choice in a few minutes. Just understand this, Johnny. This idea isn't harebrain. No, you don't want anything to do with Manie Grass. I don't blame you. Who would? But Manie Grass as an individual isn't our only concern. Sure, he'll try to rob a bank and, assuming by some miracle he succeeds, he'll attempt to rob another one. It's our job to see that he doesn't do it. And now it becomes your job to see that he doesn't."

"Crabs, Nugent, you don't need me for a lousy bank job. Fort Knox, yes, but not a bank."

"Yes, of course," said Matt, "if it were only the bank. Look, Johnny, it's the bazooka dough we want. There was a half million dollars of that stuff lifted from the armored truck and when you lose a big chunk like that people get itchy about its whereabouts. Manie has it. You're going to get it."

Suddenly his eyes were beaded like birdshot. "And you can. Let's look at it this way. If you can fake your way past Patty Sears this afternoon—a friend of Renney's— you certainly can fake it in the presence of people who never saw you before. So what happens? To oversimplify things, you pile into Ogsinto, Apple Renney, the big wheel

27

from the coast. You offer fifty cents on the dollar for the dough. If that's not enough, you can climb to sixty. Under normal circumstances you could go as high as eight-five, but not this time. The money's too hot and, personally, what with Manie stiting on it for all this time, I think he'll jump at it. After you make your pitch, you arrange a meet between him and the top bananas in the California syndicate. We become the syndicate. We take over."

I hadn't realized that I had suddenly become interested. "What about this thirty thousand you mentioned before?"

"That's your cut. It's actually the reward put up by the insurance company. There're no strings, Johnny. We'll have the company confirm it today."

I said slowly, "I join up with Grass, win his confidence, arrange a meet, then when the lobsters arrive, run like blazes for the hinterlands. Is that it?"

"That's it."

"How do I get off the hook?"

Matt nodded toward Crypt Number Ten. "He's your hook. After it's over we release the news that Renney is dead. Nobody will know any different."

"Except this one little loving family."

"It's a family you can trust."

"It's a family I have to trust. What about those two gorillas?"

"They're not gorillas," said Matt glibly, "and they're not attendants, either. They're two of my best men."

"In other words," I said, "except for Agnes, only the police know about this."

"Right."

I gave myself a few moments to digest Matt's words. "All right," I said, "my job basically is to get the half million back. But what happens about this bank job you

28

think they have planned?"

"The bank job," confirmed Matt, "will never come off. If you're successful with your part, that's the end of it and—" he went on quickly—"if by some chance it does come off, we'll be waiting for them."

"That might be tricky," I said. "I'll have to let you know the exact date and time of the robbery."

Matt nodded. "Yes, it might be tricky, but I don't think there's much to worry about. Remember, you're the wheel. You're the expert, transported from the coast to assist in a bank robbery because you're smart. You're also 'Mr. Big.' You have a reputation over and above Manie's, for the simple reason that you're playing ball in a better league. You're not the one who'll listen to him. You'll tell him what's going to happen. You'll tell him when the bank will be robbed."

"All right," I said, "it's getting better. I look like Renney and, after your staff works on my features, I might be able to pull it off. But what proof do you have that Renney never met Manie Grass?"

"The letter we found on Renny."

I stretched my arm. "Give."

He handed it over and I pored over the pidgin English which had been formed with a crude and unsure hand. Matt was right. It was apparent that Manie and Apple were strangers. And it was also apparent that something hot was cooking. No bank job was mentioned directly, but the inference was there.

What else could it mean? Manie knew no other occupation.

Matt prodded me. "You'll go up?"

I didn't move and I didn't lift my head. "I don't know. Wait until I see Patty Sears. If I can get by him—well, we'll see."

29

SO LOVELY TO KILL

Matt was himself again and his stomach made like jelly. This exuberance remained when the door swung open and Agnes maneuvered her trim body back into the room. She looked like an aesthetic ballet dancer toeing down an unaesthetic burly runway and she dragged in her wake the attendant who had absconded with my trousers and a sloppy little gent whose unshaven face was naked with fear. His clothes were baggy and dirty and he wore cantaloupes for eyes. He did not choose to advance far into the dreary cavern. He stood just inside the door, limbs shaking so violently that they were almost a blur.

"This," announced Anges, "is the tattoo man, Louis. That is your name, isn't it?"

Little Louis took one step forward and said hesitantly, "Y-yes, Louis, and Louis no want job. Me give twenty dollar back. Here, take. Louis no want."

I felt sorry for the runt and might have tried to console him had not Agnes gone to Crypt Number Ten, twisted the handle and hauled out the drawer. Exposed once again was the lifeless form of one departed gangster, Charles Apple Renney.

Matt's man took over and we watched in silence. He grabbed the body by one arm and one leg and deftly, with the practiced skill of a weight lifter, heaved it over on its stomach. I turned my head away. It was sickening. It affected Louis the same way, possibly more, because I suddenly became concerned with the significance of it all. I had a sneaky feeling . . .

I was right. My gaze settled on the body and I exclaimed, "Oh, God. No!"

"It will be only temporary," said Matt assuringly. "Only temporary. Louis," he called, "tell the man that the tattoo will be temporary."

Louis confirmed it with a nod, a shrug and a wave of

his pale hands. "It last five, maybe six week. But, honest, Louis no want job. Hand shake too much."

"Get him a drink," Matt said to Agnes and she complied immediately. She pulled a bottle and a glass from the desk drawer and poured the tremulous skin artist four fingers of burning hooch.

I said nothing. Transfixed, I surveyed the backside of Renney's body. There, colored a vivid red, was a birthmark and it was the size and shape of a juicy, succulent apple. Hence the man's peculiar nickname.

"Temporary," I muttered. "You sure?"

"Positive," said Matt. "Right, Louis?"

There was no reply.

"Right, Louis?"

We turned and looked at the man. He was drinking out of the bottle.

31

4

AT 10:16 A.M. Matt and I arrived at police headquarters and I made like a school boy for the rest of the day. Honestly, I don't think I ever studied harder in all my life and this would include the sum total of cramming hours from kindergarten on through college. Not only did I devour everything available about Apple Renney, but I studied his friends, even muggs he knew only casually. I read and read and listened and listened and got wearier by the hour. We kept a line open with the L.A. police for half the day and they helped immensely and with enthusiasm. They were doing flips, having learned that the California bad boy, Renney, was dead.

Of more help was an East-side stoolie owning the incongruous name of Cedric Churchill, about as English looking as the Mayor of Stalingrad. He was virtually in the employ of the police department, had welched on so many buddies, and looked like the type who'd sell out his mother for a candy bar. He was bald and had a beet-red face and he was always smiling, trying to make you think that he was something and you were dirt. He wasn't to be trusted. But Matt trusted him and I trusted him because there was nothing else to do.

Cedric was my voice instructor.

"Higher, Mr. Fury, higher," Cedric implored. "Mr.

32

SO LOVELY TO KILL

Renney has—or had—a voice like yours but higher."

I worked like hell on it and didn't get it. It just wasn't there. The tone was okay, if you could trust Cedric's word for it, but the inflections and dialect weren't even in the ball park.

"Don't be so polite when you say something, Mr. Fury. Be rough and a little higher."

"How the hell can you be rough and higher at the same time?"

Cedric would shrug and off we would go on another session.

Finally, I figured out what was wrong. Cedric was an East-sider, as Renney once had been, and theirs is a dialect as distinctive as anything found anywhere. I gave it the "toid" and "foist" and "woild" and then—because Renney had been away from his native pavements for years— softened my pronunciations slightly, adding the faintest touch of Coast twang. It worked and Cedric was beaming, thinking that soon his job would be done and he would be going home. But he was not going anywhere. He was to be kept on ice until my job was finished. Rough, perhaps, and certainly illegal, but that is what happens to guys who take up the occupation of stooling.

While Cedric and I had been batting the English language around, I had been sitting in a chair and two guys were working me over like surgeons. My mustache came off, and I was glad to lose it. My hair became a gaudy yellow instead of reddish, and flesh-colored plastic was molded on my ears, making the lobes more prominent and forcing the ears out and away from my head. I was surprised to find that the plastic was soft to the touch, but I didn't know how the hell I'd get it off when my mission was accomplished. Since I already had the crazy tattoo, I was all set.

33

SO LOVELY TO KILL

So at 5:11 P.M. it began. I dragged myself to the patrol car and it hustled me to the city prison for my test—my one and only test—with the fixer, Patty Sears.

The gloom impressed me most when I arrived. It always does, in all prisons. There is an evenness of dullness, a complaining, sullen sobriety that covers the world like a pall. Even the men who sit behind the bars or stroll in the yard appear to be husked of vitality. There is no outside. The inmates are automatons, spiritless things who sluggishly breathe, work, eat, sleep and dream.

Then there are the sounds and they are different from anything imaginable. A laugh, and one is heard often enough, manages to sound as incarcerated as the body and the echo falls with a thud. Footsteps tramp through the brain, though they might be in some unseen hallway more than a block away.

There is the metallic clanging of cell doors, a man's hollow cough, sounding like a growl belched from a subterranean cave, the low rumble of meaningless conversation and each voice contributes to a riot of discord.

The guard led the way down the long corridor, past the resentful yet inquisitive stares of inmates who sat or stood in their cells. I said nothing and occasionally flicked my eyes to the right to catch an expression, a sentiment— once to smile and get a sneer for my graciousness.

It was a varied group and all were transient. Some were waiting for trial. Others had finished with that and were waiting to be transferred to the state prison. Some were just there for a nap, like the drunks and vagrants. One or two were neither happy nor sad because they defaulted on alimony payments. A dozen or so were waiting to be arraigned.

Patty Sears belonged to the last classification. He had been pulled in on a manslaughter charge. It wouldn't

34

stick, nor was it designed to. It was simply a subterfuge to keep him there long enough for me to see him—and for him to see me.

Hence, it was Operation Testing. If I passed, fine. If I failed? Well, what the hell. No thirty thousand. Just the same old John Fury, who looks like a dead-end hood, and nothing could be lost, except the loss civilization suffers when a claw like Manie Grass is permitted to cavort as free as a summer cloud.

Metal plates on the guard's shoes set up the major beat; my rubber heels added the thud and this *clank-thump, clank-thump* was the obnoxious little song our feet made as we moved down the cell block.

Then, breaking the rhythm was a wild greeting.

"Apple! Hi' ya, Apple! What you doing in New York?"

I couldn't miss the guy. He was the shape, if not the size of an elephant. He hung on the bars of his cell, dancing now on one foot, then on the other. He wasn't Patty Sears.

I forced a smile. "Visiting. How you doing?" and continued walking.

"Good. You visiting here, too?" he said.

"Yeah."

"Best way to do it. Best. How's the chest?"

"Better."

"Good. You're looking swell."

"See you, boy."

"Yeah, see you back in sunny L.A." He laughed.

He was too burly and his lips were bulbous, spread all over his fat face when he smiled.

I didn't glance back. I steeled my eyes straight ahead, aware that my stomach was rolling.

He had called me "Apple". He thought I was Renney and that was all there was to it. I had no misgivings, I

35

could have patted myself on the back for not forgetting the voice, even though this guy's greeting seemed suddenly to pop out of the wall.

I wondered, then, why it hadn't happened before—before I was expertly disguised. After all, if I looked like Renney, fate might have arranged a mistaken identity at least once. On the other hand, why? There're over a hundred and fifty million people in this country and, unless you're a celebrity, you can get lost in a hurry—forever. Renney wasn't that important, and his business called for a lost identity. Still, I couldn't shake that gnawing feeling. Coincidence was an avalanche, tumbling down on me, all in one day. I searched my brain. Had anyone ever called me Apple before? I couldn't recall. Maybe I had been hanging out with another class of people.

I turned to the guard. "Who's fat stuff?"

"A bookie. Gruber's his name."

"From here? The city?"

"California, some place. This is his welcome party." The guard turned his sour face. "The jerk. He's not in town two hours and he's taking bets like he owned all Manhattan and Queens. We'll ship him off quick. We got enough books of our own."

I figured that Gruber's head was on a rusty rocker. No bookie plops his big fat business in New York and starts to operate—not for long anyway, because that sort of daring is frowned upon by the syndicate. Gruber was a stupe.

But in a way his being there was a break. If Gruber started to talk, once he was out, he would confirm that Renney had visited Patty Sears.

The guard gave me the sign and I slackened my pace. He drifted ahead and I stayed out of sight until he inserted the key, turned it and slid the heavy barred door into the slot in the wall. He nodded to me and my mind recited that classic remark made by the virgin bride. "Well, this is it. . . ."

Only I didn't blush.

I shuffled in.

Patty Sears was small and thin, his head the size of an unripe cocoanut and his two floppy ears could have been rented out by ad men. His was a putty face, having no distinction, like any one of the fabulous herd who tramp pavements, push pencils or plow fields. Not handsome, not homely, just a face that remained blank—until he saw me.

"Apple, you licker of lollipops," he yelped, though he didn't say it that way. His choice of words was slightly more earthy. "How the hell did you get in here?"

He had a nervous, high-pitched voice and I judged him to be fifty. His grin was clownlike in its enthusiasm.

I played it affably. "I just asked and they let me in."

"The hell you say."

"It's the truth, so help me."

"Gee, I never expected—"

There were two bunks, so I sat down on one. Patty took the other.

The guard closed the cell door and, playing his part well, announced, "Five minutes, punk, and don't cause no trouble."

"Gee," said Patty Sears, "how'd you hear I was here?"

"In the Bronx last night—or, rather, this noon. I just happened to overhear it in a bar."

"Gee, so soon they know." He laughed. "Say, you're a real pal coming to see me. For a while there I didn't think you'd spit on me."

"I know my friends," I said.

I played it straight, my manner as neutral as a capon's.

37

Not too many smiles, not too many frowns, and I couldn't have guessed wrong, because Patty didn't flicker an eyelash.

He said, whining, "How do you like this," indicating the drab interior of the tiny cell. "They say I ran over a guy in my car last night. Gee, last night I didn't even have my car. Last night I was shacking up with Esther."

"You didn't do it?"

"Nuts! I didn't do nothing. She'll tell them. She owes me plenty of favors. Besides, everyone knows we plunk around now and then." He added frankly: "And if she don't tell them, I'll fan her."

I smiled. "You contact your shyster yet?"

Rocking his head from side to side, he moaned, "Hell, yes, but they can keep you frozen for a while. It's a nuisance."

Patty Sears dismissed his own woes and leaned forward. After making a furtive inspection of the corridor, he asked, "You going up?"

"Tonight," I said.

He frowned and fell back against the wall, his skinny arms folded like sticks across his puny chest. "I wish you luck, Apple. You'll need it."

"Why, is he hard to work with?"

His lip curled. "Nah, you and him'll get along. It might work real good. You got brains, he got the muscle, and if he has the Marchetti brothers there you'll be okay." He tapped his head with his index finger. "They're kind of slow, but cool. Real cool."

"Well, what do I have to worry about?"

"I told you."

"So I forgot," I said and slipped in the rough inflection.

"So how can you forget such a thing?" His voice wasn't mean. It was a polite reprimand.

38

SO LOVELY TO KILL

"You tell me a lot of things," I said. "What are you talking about?"

"His wife, Dee."

"Oh," I intoned, making believe I remembered.

Fortunately, he didn't drop it. "She's at that age, you know. Still has looks, but wants to try them out once in a while. Really try them out. Manie's got an obsession about that."

I nodded, said nothing.

"And don't fiddle with Carol, either."

I said I wouldn't. Carol was Manie's daughter by a previous marriage. This was another chapter I had memorized during the morning and afternoon. But I couldn't elaborate, not on a thing, except, maybe, that I wore a size sixteen shirt and try to slip that into a conversation.

Carol, I had learned, was twenty-three and pretty. She had the benefit of two or three years of good schooling and she might have elevated herself to a decent position in the world had not the bazooka trial exposed her identity. I made a note to stay clear of both women.

"This Causby farm in Ogsinto," I said. "What's it like?"

Patty's face became pained. "What's the matter, you sick or something?"

"I've been sick," I said. "Pneumonia."

"What did it do—affect your mind? I told you weeks ago."

I shrugged. "Those drugs they give you. They make you dull."

"Well, you better get bright fast. Manie ain't patient, you know." He exposed his palms and breathed deeply. "I still don't know why you want in with him. You got a good setup on the coast."

I leveled my finger at him. "Look, Patty, just don't

ask too many questions."

He melted. "Sure, Apple, you know me."

The guard returned. He opened the door, giving me access to what seemed like a universe of spaciousness outside the cell. Still in good form, he said casually, "Your time's up. Out!"

I stood. I offered my hand and Patty grabbed it. He seemed happy that I didn't grind him like dirt.

"Give my regards to M," he said.

"I'll do that and thanks for your help."

His grin spread like a rash. "Sure, Apple, you know me."

I beat it, trying not to seem in a hurry.

5

DID IT COME off? I was sure it had. I hopped in the patrol car, told the driver to stash the chatter and juggled it around in my mind as we bucked the evening traffic en route to lobster headquarters.

When I strode into Matt's office, Agnes was there. She was wearing a chic black satin cocktail dress, the kind that makes mere words seem silly. It showed off a bust that would battle to escape any garment not reinforced with steel and concrete. The rest of her was aptly proportioned, too. Especially her rocking little hips. All together now. Follow the bouncing ball.

She said, "Hi, Johnny," and her tone was serious. She was like that, mildly dizzy one minute, pensive the next. She was eyewash for my tired eyes and I felt like kissing her, forgetting about the psychological block that made me revolt at the touch of her hands. I think at that moment I could have pulled if off without a shudder. I didn't.

Matt's thick finger was scratching up and down the side of his nose. He said, "The guard just called. Patty acted the same after you left. Nothing strange."

"Good," I said.

"Do you think you graduated?"

I nodded. "I think so. He might think I'm a little off, but that's all. To him I'm Apple Renney."

41

"You're on then?" He sounded wistful.

"About that I'm not sure," I said with conviction and then smiled. "But if I am, it's just for a lark."

He corrected me with a rumbling laugh, "And thirty thousand smackers."

"Yeah," and we all laughed, but it was more a nervous release. Oh, it had been done before, a million times, I guess. A guy impersonates another guy for dough and, it shouldn't be forgotten, justice, too—a factor not ignored by decent people. Even I had done it before, during the war, but then I had been impersonating a Frenchman— any Frenchman. I had not been required to assume a voice, a character, a personality or the habits of a particular person.

Agnes stepped between us and said to Matt, "Don't worry about Johnny, Matt. He'll go up. I'll see to that."

Matt made a joke of it. "Sure, maybe you'd like to share that thirty thousand, too."

Agnes said nothing and neither did I. Such remarks plainly disturbed me. This pretty gal was a-chasing.

Matt handed over to me Renney's wallet, the usual miscellaneous junk a man carries and a thin wad of expense money. I jammed everything into my pockets and stood there.

There was nothing more to say. All had been said and had I chosen to spend the few remaining hours cramming more facts into a weary and loaded brain I might have turned a clear broth into an Irish stew. I was as well prepared as could be expected.

Agnes stood, brushed her hips down and a cute wiggle helped her get rid of imaginary wrinkles. "Come on, Johnny, we'll get dinner."

"I didn't know I invited you."

Her bewitching smile. "You didn't. I'm inviting you."

"Good idea," said Matt happily. He rubbed his hands together. "I think I'll come along."

He was set straight in a hurry. "You, my dear Lieutenant, can go soak your head." It wasn't me who said that. It was Agnes.

At dinner I picked at my food. My stomach was tight and shunned nourishment, but whipped along by Agnes I managed to get something down.

Agnes tried to amuse me and the spiciest diversion came when she leaned forward to burn her big, black peepers into mine. They were as dark and mysterious and turbulent as fifty fathoms of midnight ocean. Her hand ensnared my wrist and I forgot about my phobia—or didn't care. This was a woman, one who would become mine if I wanted her. Maybe she was mine already. I didn't know.

She said softly, "Are you worried, Johnny?"

"Nothing to it."

"You're not a criminal investigator," she said flatly and the smouldering heat of her tone was gone. She was the cool, practical woman again.

"What are you talking about?"

"I mean that you do so little of it."

She was right, of course, but how many private dicks get involved in the cloak and dagger aspect of criminal work? Actually, very few. The bona fide, licensed operator leaves the dirty work to the cops. There's a good reason for it. No dough. I had found that my most lucrative dodge was supplying divorce evidence. Oh, sometime it makes you want to heave, but what can do? Refuse a job and your reputation is nil among the lousy little people who have most use for a private eye. Lately the shoplifting service was bringing my growing concern a tidy little income. Actually, few shoplifters are apprehended, but the signs that are posted, stating that the

43

store subscribes to the John Fury Detective Service, acts as a deterrent to petty thievery and gives a boost to store morale. They also advertise John Fury. Guarding bodies, ferreting missing persons, installing alarm systems, spying on an erring spouse, and character investigations just about cover the whole business, and that's what it is when you face up to it. A business.

Teaming up with bank robbers, sanctioned or not, was not a normal part of my routine and this was what Agnes was jabbering about. She was saying as gaily as a school girl, ". . . and if the bank robbery does come off, how much money do you think you'd be able to get?"

I guess I blew my top because I told her to stack it, not wanting to think about it. I knew that for days or weeks or maybe months, I would do nothing but eat, drink and sleep it. I must have spoken pretty harshly, because she became moody and a five-year old would have known that we were on edge.

I'm not inconsiderate, so I apologized.

She said, "It's all right, Johnny. You're worried, but you'll make out fine and come home with bells on."

"Yeah, cowbells."

She winked at me. "Any kind of bells. I just love the sound of bells."

She leaned forward and grasped my hand and my neat little play at repentance was shot because, as though on schedule, I recoiled at her touch. It was those damn corpse-tossing hands!

"Why don't you get out of that racket?" I erupted.

She didn't take the bait, if that was what I was throwing at her. She withdrew her hand and said evenly, "I'm a medical technician and I'm fitted for it. I like my work and until I don't have to work any more I will continue to do it."

SO LOVELY TO KILL

If that wasn't a straight line for a proposal to marriage
I never heard one. I let it gallop past like a runaway horse.
I just sat there, a glum, obstinate, heartless glob of ecto-
plasm.

I guess Agnes had had enough, because she put her napkin on the table and suggested, "It's eight-thirty, Johnny.
I think we should be going."

The evening had turned into a wake and Agnes, I re-
discovered, was quite capable of dousing me with her own
particular brand of coldness. I could have surrendered to
the mood, said, "Sure," and taken her home. I didn't. I
called the waiter, ordered two more drinks, pushed my
chair back and said, "Come on, baby, let's dance. We're
acting like—" I almost said an old married couple—
"children."

She didn't answer. She led the way to the dance floor,
turned around and fell into my arms. She pressed close
against me, as she had never done before.

Immediately, the beetles were chased away. We felt better. I don't know why. And I don't know if the reaction was
mental or physical. I suppose it was mostly physical. After
all, what she wore—and didn't—could do something to a
guy. And, of course, there was the warmth of motion and
music, and a nebulous feeling that we really didn't want
to be angry with one another.

Our dining place was the restaurant in one of Times
Square's better hotels. The orchestra had too many fid-
dles and played scratchily, but the lights were low, which
I liked, because I didn't want it blown around that Apple
Renney was dancing with what the uninformed underworld might consider the equivalent of a cop—the motif
was subdued, the antithesis of the general noise and
grime of Manhattan.

Only a few others were dancing. That helped, too. We

were alone and together and nuts to the rest of the world.

"Johnny?" Agnes whispered with her rich lips parted. Her breath was like perfume.

"Huh?"

"This time I'm not asking you. I'm insisting. You will take care of yourself and you will come home."

Since it wasn't said maternally, I didn't mind. "Uh-huh."

She sighed, wiggled. "I'll quit my job if you want me to."

I wavered, wanting and not wanting, and finally managed to postpone it. "You like your work, baby."

She wavered, too. "I know." And, damn it all, I had to believe her.

I did believe in the correctness of what happened next. She pressed closer. My arms tightened around her and something leaped back and forth between us, making us vulnerable. I cocked my head and my lips caught her beneath the ear and, if it was a suggestion I wanted, I got it.

"Johnny, honey?"

"Yes."

"We'll go to your apartment."

"Yes."

"To pack," she added.

Sure, to pack. Why not? I was the businessman, working for money.

I let her start packing for me. From my stall shower, I bellowed instructions. I knew she'd do it well—no big, telltale mistakes. After all, she was part cop herself. For another thing, my clothes could fit any occasion. I wore nothing monogrammed and, since I was a bachelor, nobody ever got around to putting name labels in my shirts.

"Your suitcases, where are they?" she called.

"In the closet."

"One is initialed."

"I know. It's a gift from my mother. Forget that one."
There was silence for a while. "That leaves only the big one."

"Pack it hard," I shouted. "Use muscle."

Another silence. "I'll let you use yours."

I came out of the shower and began to use the towel. I was preoccupied—my mind sliding from thought to thought, some important, some not, all concerned with the hood, Manie Grass. I felt nervous, but I was used to that. In Counter Intelligence, during the war, I had faced every new assignment with trepidation—sometimes with actual nausea. But as soon as I got into the work, all that had vanished under the feeling that what I was doing was worth while.

In regard to Manie Grass and his playmates, would I feel the same way? If this caper worked, I could at least think of myself as a garbage man, tying up and carting away the dregs of society . . .

"Johnny?" Agnes called.

"Huh?"

"May I come in?"

"You stay where you are." I sounded disgusting like a typical, bashful male.

"I just want to see your tattoo."

Cripes, I had forgotten about it. I dropped the towel and inspected myself in the mirror. There it was, all right, like on a tree, juicy, red and round. It was just waiting to be plucked and I felt foolish staring at it.

"What does it look like?" called Agnes.

"Very much like an apple," I said.

"I'd sure love to see it."

"I'm sure glad you're not going to."

47

"Well, some day I'll get hunk on you, boy. I'll take a big bite out of it."

The suggestion made my flesh crawl. I think, pleasantly.

"Johnny?"

"Huh?"

"It's after nine."

"Coming."

I jockeyed into my shorts and trousers, socks and shoes, then discovered that I had forgotten my undershirt. Nude from the waist up, I entered my bedroom.

It was nothing. It happened every day.

No, check that. It was something. It had never happened before. The effect was electric, first on Agnes, then on me. There was a woman, a gorgeous, scrumptious lassie, dutifully doing a personal thing, like helping a husband get off on a business trip. There was a man, young, strong, vibrantly alive and aware of himself as body, as flesh, as blood—a man dressing and staring at the woman.

She dropped her eyes as demurely as a virgin—she probably was one—and in an instant all the hot-shot talk was gone. She seemed almost a child, not quite sure of herself or the world or what she should do. Phony sophistication was eradicated and something—a tenderness— took its place.

For only a second I hesitated, then went to her and bundled her in my arms. Her lips yielded immediately, hungrily, and I heard the whisper of her breath when finally it ended. She trembled. I think I did, too. I kissed her again and nails scraped across my bare back.

"Johnny?"

"Yes, baby."

She was unsure. "I—I really don't want you to go."

"I'll be all right," I said emphatically.

"Promise?"

"I promise." I kissed her again, then released her and went to the dresser for the undershirt.

It was the wrong thing to do, a knack all men have, but one I've mastered to the point of infallibility.

Her face flushed scarlet and her eyes were licking flames. "What's wrong," she snapped and her voice was unsteady.

"Huh?"

"Am I that ugly?"

I had a feeling I knew what she was talking about and went to her again. She spun away and sank her face into the draperies at the window. Wrathful sobs shook her. I put my hand on her waist and tried to turn her around.

She twisted free. "Don't touch me!"

I flapped my arms against the sides of my legs and frowned.

"Why?"

"Because maybe I don't like your hands either. Did you ever think of that?"

She wasn't acting. Something had her hopped up. She strode to the bed, grabbed her jacket and handbag and spun toward the door. I intercepted her and held her arms. I said nothing. She was the one who was angry.

She raised her eyes to mine and she was still seething. "I'm a woman. I'm here in your apartment. Doesn't that suggest anything to you?"

Then, and only then, I got the whole picture. I wasn't following the rules. As the age-old game is played, I was supposed to make a play for her and she was supposed to resist me. I would fail, of course, and the only outlet for my frustration would be marriage.

Hah!

"Look," I said. "If I tried anything you'd scream bloody murder."

49

Her eyes narrowed, bright and cold. "At least you could have tried."

She broke free and ran out of the apartment. The door slammed, shaking the room, and I stared at the void.

I thought I had messed things. Before, I was worried because I had a woman. Now I was worried because I didn't have one, and it occurred to me that maybe she hadn't been playing a game, that maybe . . .

I started after her, stopped. A small *snap* in my mind reminded me that I had hold of something far more important than the woman scorned. I strode back to the dresser, yanked out an undershirt and pulled it on.

I had to take it off and put on another one. The first one tore.

6

I LEFT the city moodily and in bad temper. My world had become a futile place and each second I lived was a snare.

I bought an *Esquire* from a passing huckster, slouched in the coach chair and started to read. Read? Aggie was playing leap frog in my brain. Every once in a while she pranced up to me and stroked my face with her hands. In my daydreams I didn't mind it at all. All that seemed to prove was that I was neurotic. Or was I? With a successful mission behind me, I'd have the nest egg—and Agnes and, except for those unbearable hands, she had all the equipment. Brother, when she wiggled I heard tomtoms!

The confusion stayed with me as the train huffed out of the station and into the somnolent countryside north of the city. It wasn't until we were within braking distance of Ogsinto that my turbulence was mollified. My concentration shifted to the business at hand. Why not? This was a hot assignment and my ability to keep alert would go a long way to keep me alive.

At the station I hailed a cab.

I said, "Do you know where the Causby place is?"

The young, moon-faced cabby frowned. "You want to go there?"

"I wouldn't have asked if I didn't."

51

SO LOVELY TO KILL

"Sure, mister, hop in, but you got yourself a ride."

He wasn't whistling *Pagliacci*. I spent a good twenty minutes bouncing over the bumpy country roads. Ogsinto, I found, was a busy community set in minor hills. Not ornate, not opulent, but a practical sort of place which provided the barest needs for guests and tourists who came to bathe in the cool lakes and streams, sop up sun or stare at clear skies. Even at this hour there was a flurry of liveliness. Small night spots seemed to be bustling with revelers and dark, foliage-covered nooks undoubtedly sheltered young lovers.

That was in and around the town. We traveled far from its core, into the sparsely-settled countryside. Toward the end of the ride I asked the hackie, "What kind of a place is this Causby's?"

He said, twisting his head toward the back seat, "I don't know much about it. He keeps tourists, but I never see any of them. He also farms."

"Farms what?"

"Hell, mister, you got me."

"Know any of the guests?"

The kid didn't answer right away. "Are you a friend of Causby's, mister—relative or something?"

"I don't know Causby or his guests."

"Well," he said sheepishly. "I wouldn't have said anything, if you did, but there's one gal there." He whistled. "Brother, a bitch!"

"You know her well?"

"I don't know her at all. A while back—a month or so ago—I drove her out. She's sitting in the back, just like you, and I start a conversation. Nothing wrong, you know —just chatter, but I guess I must have said something, because all of a sudden she reaches up to the front seat and plants a doosie on my cheek and then scrapes her nails

52

into my skin. For no reason at all! Christ, did I burn! I stopped the cab and, so help me, I was all set to loosen some of her teeth when I remember it's bad for business to knock lady customers around. So I forget it and don't say another word until we get to Causby's." He cocked his head philosophically. "And then what happens? The fare is two bucks—with a ten-buck tip. Right then I figure she can slap me around anytime she wants to. She's still a bitch, though."

"You're not getting any ten bucks from me," I said.

"Heck, mister, I ain't taking any socks from you, either."

"Was she a woman in her thirties? Dark hair, big?"

"This babe? Nah, she was small and blondlike, a real knockout. You know, one of them big city sirenes."

"Yeah, I know."

"Well, if you don't, you soon will, mister."

"We're there?"

"Yes, sir."

I couldn't see that we were anywhere, except on a desolate road, enveloped by black night and surrounded by brooding branches of trees.

I piled out of the car, gave the kid five bucks and told him to keep the change. "Which way?" I asked him.

He pointed. "Path's right there."

I peered into the ebony and did see a path sliced into a jungle of thick vegetation. I also saw a small, weather-beaten sign: CAUSBY—TOURISTS—about as inviting as the entrance to a leper colony.

"You'll see the house as soon as you start to walk."

I thanked him and watched him back up, turn, accelerate and disappear around the bend in the black macadam road. Soon the sound of his taxi was a whisper, then nothing, and I was alone.

SO LOVELY TO KILL

He had been right about the house. I plunged forward and found that the trees were no more than a facade. Behind them the land spread out generously and in the middle of the clearing was the house. Mellow squares of light poured from the first story windows. I stopped, took stock and was appalled.

The house was old, decrepit. It stood cold against the night sky, its eaves sagging promiscuously even in this light, its crooked chimneys pointing skyward like rheumatic fingers. Around me was the insect chorus, madly chirping its approval of the season. There was no discernible breeze, yet the air was sluiced with fragrance. I wasn't sure, but it smelled like cider.

I stepped forward again, then stopped. The front door to the farmhouse opened, and the surrounding area was flooded with yellow light. A wizened old creature, moving swiftly, though with effort, came to meet me. Cradled in his arms was a shotgun.

About ten feet away he stopped and leveled the gun at my middle. I doubt that I breathed.

"What do you want?" Simple and direct. His voice was dry and crackled like autumn leaves.

"I'm—" I caught myself. I almost gave him my name. Something about the place, its corrupt hostility, had nearly stagnated my brain. I had to remember I was Apple Renney now. This was the start of the merry masquerade.

"I'm Renney," I said.

"You sure?"

"What the hell do you think?"

He lowered the gun and laughed. "Some late, ain't you buddy?"

"Renney," I said. "Not buddy. Not ever buddy to you, old man."

He looked me over carefully, then nodded over his

narrow shoulder and started for the house. He was a seedy, smelly creature and, as we neared the lights, I saw that his right eye was clouded with a heavy cataract. I doubted he could have hit anything with the 12-gauge he carried. He seemed to read minds also, for suddenly he broke the gun to show me it wasn't loaded.

"To scare people," he told me blandly. "It scares them to hell and back."

He was enough, old as he was. I stopped him with a hand on his arm, there under the lights. "Who the hell are you?" I asked.

"Causby. That's the last name. Nesbit's the first. I live here. I farm." He added cynically, "I take in tourists, too."

"Who've you got tonight?"

"Only Manie's wife and daughter. Hot one, she is. If I wasn't so damned old!"

"Which one?"

"His wife."

"Where's Manie?"

"Went to Willisburg to pick up the Marchetti brothers. Back soon."

I emitted an inward sigh. Better this way. I could meet one little group at a time. There'd be less of a chance to foul up.

We climbed the steps and they quivered under our weight. He kicked open the door and I maneuvered myself with my suitcase into a darkened vestibule.

The smell hit me first, a nauseating blend of garbage, manure and age. Add a cooking smell that hung over all like a rain-pregnant cloud. Everything about the place was rancid—the wood, the wall paper, which was stained and peeling, and the old-fashioned furniture.

Causby propped his gun in a corner behind the door and took my suitcase. "I'll take it up," he said tonelessly.

"You got the first room on the right. The bathroom's toward the back."

This was a service I had not expected. He nodded toward the living room and left me, puffing laboriously as he mounted the whining, complaining stairs.

I entered the living room and was jolted!

She was nude!

No, not nude. It only appeared that way—a devastating, erotic illusion. My mouth was gaping like the Lincoln Tunnel as I stood there, introducing myself as a fool.

She had no difficulty speaking. "Hello," she said immediately, breathily.

She stood in front of a long sofa. A cigarette was held daintily in her tapering fingers. She was big, like the snaps I had seen of her, but not fleshy. Few women could have looked fetching with all that bigness. She managed it like a queen, burlesque rather than royal. Her feet were encased in gold mesh slippers and flesh-colored shorts and halter covered not quite enough of her body. They were what had fooled me. A quick look could not possibly have disclosed where the material ended and she began. Her black hair was feather short, her brows dark and vivid against cameo skin and her red lips were large, heart-shaped and firm. And her bosom? Good God!

"Hi," I said finally.

"I'm Dee," she said, "and this is Carol. Carol, Mr. Renney."

"Call me Apple," I said, and I didn't feel foolish about it at all.

At first I hadn't noticed the girl. Manie's daughter was lost in the cradle of a huge, battered chair. And, as the hack driver had said, she was truly a sexy "sirene." Her body was slight, but she was not frail. Long honey-

SO LOVELY TO KILL

colored hair fell in casual waves to her shoulders. She wore a simple blue-and-white print blouse and her face was set in hard lines, her eyes hard and cold.

I had expected the opposite from what Matt had told me. I had expected Carol to be the one near-human member of a degraded household. Dee, strangely, seemed the warm one, apparently unaffected by the harshness of a life with Manie Grass.

Carol raised her eyes from her magazine and enunciated a terse, "How do you do." Her critical stare was about as pleasant as a bleeding ulcer.

"Drink, Mr. Renney—or Apple?" Dee was smiling at me as if she and I shared a secret. Her eyes were bright, the corners of her mouth winging up, relaxing, then winging upward again. I could have been wrong, but I got the impression that she was delighted.

I said yes and changed it to no. "I'd better not. I should be taking it easy."

"Just a little one?"

"Okay, just a short one."

"Ginger?"

"Soda."

She walked—check that—sleeked from the room, but when she reached the shadows of the dining room, she spun around, closed her eyes, cupped her hands over her voluptuous breasts and shook her head in a sign that could be taken only for ecstasy. I didn't know how to take it. Not quite. Was she starting already? On me? I remembered what Patty Sears had said: *"She's at that age, you know . . ."*

I returned a conservative smile and she squirmed away. Carol hadn't seen the exhibition.

I said, "Been here long?"

Her eyes didn't leave the magazine. "Long enough, Mr.

57

Renney." Her voice could have chilled the August sun.

"Like it?" I tried to sound reasonably cordial, but did not think I was succeeding. A resentment had crept into my manner because, the fact was, I did not think I was going to like the girl.

"How can you like a dump like this?" she said. "On the other hand, Mr. Renney," this time she allowed me to recoil at her frigid stare—"I'm not sure what you are used to."

I said quietly, "I'm not used to this," and she could have taken it either way.

Dee bounced back with two drinks. Hers was a whopper, tall and cold and tinkling with ice. She was a whopper, too, everything about her. And when she leaned forward to hand me mine I sensed a warning constriction in my middle. It was not going to be easy to keep away from this woman—she looked like the type who would chase.

"Don't mind Carol," she said, winking at me. "She's a little edgy tonight. I think it's the Marchettis and I don't blame her. They're from hunger as far as human beings go."

I didn't answer. Neither did Carol.

The door squeaked open and I thought, *Here they come—Manie and his boy friends.* They didn't. It was Causby. He rasped at no one in particular, "I'm going to bed."

"Well, go to bed," snapped Carol. "Do you want us to tuck you in?"

Causby ignored her—he was a wise old codger—and said to Dee, "Tell Manie to lock up when he comes in."

He trudged through the living room, the dining room, to the kitchen. I guessed he slept there. No good nights were exchanged.

SO LOVELY TO KILL

I was left the object of Carol's hate. That's what it was, basically—a true loathing for everything, everyone— even, I sensed, for herself. Already I could detect the pattern. She seethed inwardly, continuously erupting without warning, spitting her wrath at anyone who happened to be around. A girl so young, so pretty. It was a shame.

She said, "I live in the barn, Mr. Renney. I have a cozy little room on the second floor, away from everyone. There's a big bolt on my door and I sleep with an axe under my pillow. Do you understand?"

I didn't bother to reply. What could a man say?

"Oh, honey, take it easy," said Dee, but she wasn't looking at Carol. Her wide eyes were transfixed on me and I thought that her pent-up warmth was getting ready to explode. She was on the verge of something, some emotion which, for the minute, was being painfully controlled.

What all this suggested had no appeal for me and, fearful that Carol might go and leave the two of us alone, I decided to avoid complications.

"I think I'll take it easy—turn in," I said, placing my half-finished drink on the scratched coffee table and rising from the chair. "I've been sick. Pneumonia. I'm tired, too."

"But you'll be all right, won't you, Apple?" said Dee.

"I'll be fine," I said nodding. "It will take a couple of days. This air should do me good."

I don't think she listened to a word I said. Her mouth opened and she aped a hungry child getting ready to suck on a lollipop. She winked again.

I said nothing.

I got out fast.

7

As QUICKLY as I could, I slipped out of my clothes and into my pajamas. Ordinarily, I didn't wear the things, but this was a new life. I was supposed to be recuperating from pneumonia and dressing the part would help. I also touched the plastic on my ears, nervously, just to make sure it was still there.

I inspected the room Causby had given me. It was surprisingly neat and the bed looked clean. In my lifetime I've slept in plenty of places, in many a strange bed, under circumstances both pleasant and bad. Once I had to struggle through a cold December night in a tree, another time on a hummock of rocks, with pebbles for a pillow. And there was the night in Belgium when Tina, dark and pie-eyed, bumped her way into my room, mistaking it for the general's. But that was in Belgium.

Let's just say that I prefer my nights to be unhampered by dirt, smell—or interruptions.

Of course, I still contended with the smell. The festering farm house manufactured it, but on the whole I was lucky. The rugless room was furnished with a plain mahogany dresser, a night table, a chair, a red floor lamp and two green ashtrays. There was a ceiling light and a closet. It was enough. All I wanted was sleep.

I opened the window a few more inches, pulled the

light cord and plopped on the bed languidly. I bounced once. The mattress didn't squeak and felt fairly comfortable. I pushed the thin, cotton cover to the foot and pulled the sheet over me and, after a minute, pushed that aside also. The night was warm, breathless, though not muggy—it was very still and the world outside was an omnipotent, meditating god.

I was glad I had gotten away from Dee. She bothered me. She was too eager, and her basic, unadulterated enthusiasm might be topped by a willingness to follow through. All this could lead to one thing only and a mere hint would be enough for Manie. Like that, I could predict the outcome.

Manie's reputation was bad. His mug shots and record described him as a hulking two hundred and fifteen pounder and, while he was in his forties, he reputedly did not own a ripple of flesh that was not muscle. His face was square and not unhandsome. He could have passed as a football coach or, maybe, an average, family-loving businessman. He could have, had he not been a gangster.

Yet Manie Grass was more than a gangster. He was a medical case history. And crime was not his illness. He was his own disease. At some time, many years ago, he had lost the track—perhaps before he was old enough to know that all people don't rob other people, kill them or slap them around for the pure love of hurting. How to classify his meanness? I didn't know. I'm no psychologist. I'm just a private eye who admits, occasionally, that he should have entered another profession.

The silence was broken when Carol's voice flared against the naked walls of the night. "Nice, nice!" she cried. "Why should I be nice to the bum!"

The bum was me, I knew, even though I failed to catch Dee's reply. Other words followed quickly, too faint and

61

muffled to unscramble. The spat, if that was what it was, lasted four or five minutes and ended with the slamming of the front door. It was Carol, I figured, heading for her room in the barn.

I slid out of bed and went to the window. I wanted to see how she walked. Would she be slouched and defeated when alone or would she pace defiantly, ready to fight even solitude? I saw the flashlight's frugal beam jerk through the darkness, pass somber oaks and tranquil maples. Not until she emerged from the dense shadows and into a shower of moonlight could I distinguish her shape—she walked haughtily, head high. That was good, I thought—for her there was still a chance. She was fighting.

I watched her disappear, saw a light pop on in the barn and I heard my labored breathing, exaggerated, startling—until I realized it was not all my own.

There was someone else in the room, exhaling a melody as natural and primeval as life itself.

I didn't want to turn, but had to. Who else could be there?

The answer was simple. Dee.

She stood at the doorway, the shadows playing over her, producing bewitching contrasts of light and shade. Her face was relaxed, like a drowsy puppy dog's. Puppy dog, hell! What she exuded was passion and the target was me!

"Dee," I said. My voice was supposed to sound stern.

She stepped into the room. Her arms were held away from her body, her head tilted slightly to one side and her eyes were sleepy with desire that I was desperate to understand. How could a woman turn it on so quickly for a stranger, a guy not even in the house an hour? She was, though, believe me, taking another step forward and

SO LOVELY TO KILL

she formed a picture that was both serious and funny, dangerous and desirable.

"You shouldn't be here," I said and my words sounded hollow and far away, very unmasculine—more like a protesting female preparing to fight for her honor. Honor had nothing to do with it. I was playing a part, a heavy role, and no hopped-up hotpants was going to spoil it for me. Not at the odds I faced. So I was ready, maybe to give her a swift kick where she would feel it the most— above all else, to get her out and keep her out for good. Wits I wanted. Not something wanton.

"Look, Dee—"

It did no good. She was on me, her arms tight around my neck, her pronounced womanhood flush with my body; on my lips were her lips, ravenous and burning.

I tried to push her back and spin her around. I wasn't kidding. That swift kick was still foremost in my mind, but she had become an immovable amazon and she used an unwomanly strength to retain her prey. Her rich, heady perfume choked my lungs but, believe me, there was no transmission of desire.

So it was time really to take over, time to cock my foot and plant it firmly into a target impossible to miss.

I didn't do it.

She whispered, almost crying, "Apple! Apple, darling! I thought I'd never see you again! It's been so long."

The night swallowed me. It took just one quick gulp and I felt as trapped as Jonah in the whale. The dead heat of the room blended with the flowing heat of her body. Neither, for the moment, touched me—I felt detached, unmoored, dizzy and helpless.

She must have sensed the change, felt my limbs relax and my shoulders surrender. She said quickly, "Apple, honey, what's wrong?"

63

SO LOVELY TO KILL

I didn't answer. I couldn't. Not then. But she wasn't really interested in a reply. Her lips were on mine again, her tongue a dancing ember. She hugged me close to her.

"I—I've been sick, baby," I said. "Very sick. I'm not well."

"Your honey will fix that. You haven't had enough of me!"

"Manie," I said. "What about Manie?"

She was against me, leaning on me, "To hell with Manie!"

"We can't."

"An hour, honey. He won't be back for an hour."

My knees hit the bed and I tumbled backwards and, in my panic, I was aware only of violence. It was a reckless, relentless frenzy, all motion and madness. Her fingers were ten daggers and she was strong. She was insatiable. She spoke words I could not understand. I only knew that Apple Renney had been a part of her life and now I was the substitute, something necessary, needed. I was also a captive, whether I liked it or not.

"I love you, Apple. I love you!"

Only a slight hesitation. "I love you, too, baby."

It was then that the front door rattled.

We knew that Manie had come home.

8

SHE REACTED like an elf, for all her size, and lost herself in the blackness of the hallway. I didn't know where she went, her room, the bathroom, where.

I reacted, too. I groped frantically for calm, for self-possession—for the identity of Apple Renney. I found a bathrobe. I waited, for what, I didn't know.

"Dee," a voice called. "Where you at?"

Calm down, I told myself. I was puffing out miniature gales. I lay down, my head sank into the pillow and I closed my eyes.

"Dee!"

"Huh?"

"Where you at?"

"In the bathroom."

"Oh." There was a pause. "Renney get here yet?" The voice was not unpleasant.

"He's asleep. He isn't well."

"He ain't well? He sick?"

Manie Grass was outside my door now.

"Nah, just getting over pneumonia or something. Why don't you leave him alone!"

I heard a door creak open and almost simultaneously Dee yelped out a staccato scream. Bare feet pattered down the hallway.

SO LOVELY TO KILL

"What the hell are you doing," Manie boomed, "running around naked?"

"I didn't know you'd bring them up," came the muffled reply.

I heard the others, then, shuffling, mumbling sounds. They sounded like jolly roustabouts, as lovable and intelligent as paleolithic apes. They would be the Marchetti brothers.

Manie decided not to leave me alone.

My door swung open and the light infused like an explosion. This didn't bother me. It was what I saw. My back was to the door—I was on my side facing the window, and beneath it, on the floor, was Dee's wispy halter.

I could have raved like a ruptured gazelle. I didn't. It had reached the other extreme, resignation. I jolted slightly, as a person sometimes does when he awakens, and rolled over.

Manie was grinning and he didn't have a bad face at all. It was a rugged face, right now wreathed in a friendly smile. But his eyes held a searching quality. They burned deep, with furtive purposes. His brown hair was thin at the top, but his body was a concrete hulk. A battleship.

"Hi," he said. "You Renney?"

"Yeah," I said. "How are things with you, Manie?"

"Good. I hear you're sick."

I tossed it off, answering quickly to keep those restless, purposive eyes on me. "I'm okay. Had a touch of pneumonia before I came. Just give me a few days in this air."

He said, "A hot night to be dressed like that. You going some place?"

"I told you I had pneumonia. I've got to be careful. I didn't figure this joint to be formal."

He grinned at that and lumbered into the room, took station at the foot of the bed. He rested his big brogan

66

on the crossbar and I felt the jar. But he was still not in line with Dee's halter.

"I wanted you to meet my friends," he said. "This is Seymour, and this is Tee-hee."

The Marchetti brothers stood, skinny and silent and mindlessly ominous, in the doorway. After a while Seymour cleared his throat in a way that came out a growl. "You're the professor, huh?" he said with a snide inflection. "The smart boy?"

I didn't reply and searched his flat, homely face. His hair was black and cut close and it looked like a short-bristled and well-used brush. His complexion was sallow, almost sickly. Both of them were young, in their late twenties, but it was Tee-hee, the shorter one, who provoked more interest. He was a rare biological specimen. Blond, with too much hair. His face wore a transfixed grin. His expression was virtually imbecilic and his blue eyes were slits. He looked sleepy.

He said, or laughed, "Tee-hee," which explained his nickname. "The smart professor."

Brothers, I thought, and wondered how such a thing could happen.

Manie rolled his thick shoulders, like a giant sea turtle. He strode over to the window and I sucked in my breath and held it.

"Did you meet Carol?" he asked.

I told him I had, hoping my voice sounded strong. Manie's big foot was crushing the halter. He never looked down.

"Her lights are still on," he said. "She should go to bed earlier. She don't get enough sleep." Real paternal, I thought. There was a tender look on Manie's craggy face. He turned back to me. "She has a bolt on her door."

"She told me."

"Good. That's all you gotta remember and we'll get along fine."

Tee-hee sniggered and Seymour growled.

No one offered a good night. They walked out of the room. Manie thoughtfully pulled the ceiling light cord.

I waited four, five, six seconds, hopped out of bed and grabbed the halter, stuffed it in a pocket of my suitcase, crawled back to bed. It was over. I had made it. The whole business had been a breeze.

A breeze? Crabs! Apple Renney and Dee had been lovers. When? Where? How long? I wondered if I would ever find out.

9

I AWOKE as Johnny Fury and saw the golden sunlight stream through the window and on the bed. I felt its caressing, penetrating warmth. A robin chattered at a merry rate in a nearby tree and was being answered raucously by a bullying jay. There was a flower scent in the air and it squelched the rotten odor of the farmhouse. The farmhouse!

Reality shattered into a million nasty pieces. The day became a squalid nightmare. I was no longer Johnny Fury. I was Apple Renney, being jostled along in the devil's parade.

The night swelled back to consciousness, the insane abandon of Dee, the near disaster when Manie made his abrupt return, the evil blotch that Causby used for an eye, the roll of Manie's shoulders, Tee-hee and his brother.

There was more. I was supposed to rob a bank. This was fact. A bank robber doesn't team up with a bank robber to play parchesi.

Of course, as Matt had said, this wasn't going to happen. Once I made a deal for the bazooka dough, I could fold my tent and slink into the nearest limbo. Let the cops do the rest—it wasn't my worry. All I wanted was thirty thousand clams for being a bright, upright man.

The door eased open and things looked about ripe to

start all over again. There stood Dee, the infidel, Apple's sweetheart, her age of thirty-five or -six summers resting lightly upon her and she damned near succeeded in bursting out of the blue sweater that draped her rebellious bosom. *No,* I thought, *not again.* Anything could happen now. It was daylight. People were up and doing.

She had something else on her mind. "Where is it?" she said nervously.

"Where's what?" I hissed back.

"My—" She hesitated.

"Oh, in the pocket of my suitcase."

Quickly she retrieved the halter, thrust it into the pocket of her wide, flaring skirt.

"I can't stay," she said shaking her head.

Good, I thought.

"But we have to get together. Maybe tonight. God, I hope tonight!"

"We will, baby. We will!"

The "baby" must have done something to her. Haste was not forgotten, but she surrendered a few seconds to drop to her knees beside the bed, burn her hands against my chest and fuse her soft lips with mine.

She breathed in my ear, "Have you figured it out yet?"

I thought, *Figured what out? Oh, yes. The bank job.*

I said, "No, not yet."

"Not yet? Honey, you have to. The sands, you know."

"What sands?"

"They're running out."

"Oh! Well, I have to wait," and I wondered how long I could keep it up—bluffing a conversation that was beyond me.

"For what?" and her eyes were wide.

"Until I see that bank, I mean."

70

SO LOVELY TO KILL

"Not the bank," she whispered firmly. "Manie! How will we kill Manie?"

"Huh?"

"Dee!" It was Manie's possessive call, beast to its mate.

"Coming!" she shouted. To me she said, "I can't stay."

This was obvious. "No, you can't."

She kissed me and was gone and I was weak again. Kill Manie! What had Matt sent me to? I thought about it, hard, and finally the answer came to me. It was simple. As far as Manie knew, I was there to work for him. Actually, I was there to kill him. The plot had been on the fire for a long time, I guessed. Apple must have made numerous trips in from the coast and had many sessions with Dee. About this there could be no doubt. And the bazooka dough? Somehow, there seemed to be a connection.

I felt I was close to something and would have liked to have thought about it more. I had no chance. Manie's pile-driving feet pounded up the stairs and I sprang from the bed. No sense looking like a deadbeat.

He came in—he had the habit, I gathered, of not knocking. If there was a door in the way, shove it open.

"Hi," he said, his grin friendly. He rolled his thick shoulders once in the habitual gesture.

"Morning, Manie." I went to my suitcase for a change of underwear and, making conversation, said, "What happens to dirty laundry around here?"

"We might not be here long enough to worry about it."

"That we have to talk about."

"Yeah, we got plenty to talk about."

He went to the window and peered out over the bright morning scene. His ocular target was the barn, his daughter, Carol, the bitch on wheels. Whatever he owned he protected well, I surmised, constantly and possessively.

71

SO LOVELY TO KILL

Maybe that was why Dee was so hopped up.

"I was wondering about the letter I wrote you," he said casually. "You got it with you?"

"Sure." I fished it out of the suitcase and gave it to him.

"No sense keeping it around," he said.

"No, best to burn it."

"Where's the envelope?"

"Burned."

"Good."

He didn't make a move to leave and I had a hunch why. I shed my pajama bottoms, turned my back and slipped into a fresh pair of shorts. He was satisfied. All he said was, "Damned funny place to have a birthmark."

"Yeah."

At breakfast we had a chance to talk. Dee served us and she did well—luscious fried eggs, the yolks of which looked like gold on platinum platters, and long slivers of aromatic bacon. At the back of the house the Marchetti brothers were playing horseshoes. They weren't good at the game. They made big, exaggerated motions and argued over close plays like frustrated baseball managers. In a nearby field Causby was puttering or digging, though I couldn't understand why. There was no evidence that the farm grew a single radish.

Manie and I got down to facts promptly and, within a minute, facts were forgotten and we were arguing like hell. With him, I discovered, spats were second nature. After confirming that it was a bank job he had in mind, he reneged when I demanded thirty-five per cent of the take. He had figured on a thirty-seventy breakdown and the five per cent difference was enough to color his face an angry shade of blue.

"Who the hell do you think you are, some big shot slob!" His voice rumbled like thunder. "This is my deal.

SO LOVELY TO KILL

I cooked it. What right you got to come in and take all the marbles."

"I got a right," I said coolly, "because you need me. If you didn't I wouldn't be here. You need me because I've never spent a day in jail. You've spent plenty. Besides, I don't see why I should have to split with a whole family, your wife and daughter, too."

This calmed him immediately and I wondered what I had said.

"Not Carol," he said, and now his voice was subdued. "She won't have anything to do with this."

"Why?"

He tried to chuckle, it didn't come off, so he shrugged his shoulders. "She's funny that way. She don't approve of her old man's profession. Dee will help, though, and she's good."

Real good and she got even better when she interrupted.

"Give him thirty-five, Manie. It's just money."

He thought about it and nodded. "All right, as a business deal."

"And I run the show."

"Just as long as you stay in line."

I nodded. "Just as long."

The bank he had in mind was in another summer resort town, Winslow, about fifty miles away.

"It's a natural," he said enthusiastically. "They got a big trotting track there and it's operating full throttle. The First National's located down the main drag, but away from the shopping section. Open?" He clapped his hands together. "They got one lousy cop directing traffic out front and he'd be easy. He looks dumber than Tee-hee or Seymour."

"Getaway?"

73

"Simple. From there on out there's only open roads."

I let him gorge himself with confidence, then asked, "What about the time?"

He seemed impatient. "Look, I cased the town for one whole month. The track closes at eleven each night and the money stays there. They put a guard over it. At nine on the dot, the next day, a patrol car brings the dough to the bank." He leaned forward. "This is what I figure—"

"I know," I said. "You figure to catch them early, before the money's stacked away."

He smiled. "Yeah," and I knew he was thinking about the bazooka dough, marked and too hot to use. In this instance, the bank officials would scarcely have time to smell the loot, much less record it.

"Okay?" he asked.

I agreed. It sounded good and I had him go over the facts again and again. This brought a surprise. Manie Grass, I found, planned poorly. He ignored detail and caution and lived by the creed of the strong right arm. It was rather frightening to listen to him and I put a stop to it fast, before more imaginary bodies plunked to the pavement.

"We do it without gunplay," I said. "Without it, do you hear!"

He shrugged.

"If it can be done."

"It can be. Things can always be done better."

"A perfectionist," he said sourly. "A big wheel perfectionist."

I said nothing, which should have indicated that I agreed, and went to the back door and bellowed at the Marchettis. Seymour dropped a horseshoe as though he had heard the voice of God. But neither moved and I had to invite them a second time to come into the house.

Still they didn't move until the master, Manie, settled it with:

"Get the hell in here."

They got and I jumped on them fast. "Can you guys be trusted to go into Winslow and do a first-class casing job without lousing it up?"

Dark-eyed Seymour took offense with a growl.

Manie said, "Go easy on them, Apple."

"Why, Manie," I said. "I haven't even started to get rough."

The Marchettis looked bewilderedly from one to the other of us. Evidently I had broken the code. The code was Manie. They were not used to being addressed directly in Manie's presence, except on Manie's authority. They waited for Manie to reassert himself.

I did, too. Manie said not a word, and presently his goons stopped looking at him. I had them, with Manie's gloweringly tacit permission.

A hitch developed when Tee-hee and Seymour admitted they couldn't drive. Manie solved it.

"I'll take them in. Got some shopping to do, anyway."

"Okay, but get back here. We've still got a lot of talking to do. What about license plates? They should have been heisted months ago."

"I got them," said Manie. "Jersey plates. I picked them up in April."

I looked him straight in the eye and forced myself to say, "You're all right, Manie. Right on the beam."

Dee sidled over and rested her hand on the side of Manie's face. "Honey," she whined, "I don't have to go with you, do I? I want to stay here and wash my hair. All right?"

Manie handled her better than I ever could have. He gave her a resounding whack on the backside and said,

75

"You go with me. We gotta get some pillowcases and it'll look better if you buy 'em. Everybody goes, except Apple. He's been sick and he gotta take it easy."

Then he blessed me with his friendly smile. For a hood, and when he wasn't arguing, he had a real affectionate nature.

10

THEIR DEPARTURE was delayed. Carol didn't want to go. I stood on the front porch and heard the wrangling spill from the second floor of the barn. Manie's voice filled the air like thunder and, interspersed, I heard Carol's more artful retaliations. She was a hellion who gave in to no one, I suspected, least of all to her father.

Manie rolled out of the barn, a volcano erupting, and piled into his gray Buick sedan. I knew why he was riled. Carol he trusted probably, but not me.

The car hurtled down the driveway, dust making a rusty swirl behind it. Then as quickly as it had accelerated, it slammed to a halt. Manie jumped out of the car and slammed the door.

I thought, *Oh, boy, the kid's going to catch it this time.*

Dee stayed in the car and her face was twisted fretfully. Seymour and Tee-hee remained in the back seat, but both were interested, like spectators at a cock fight. I took the hint and faked nonchalance. After all, it was a family affair.

I figured wrong. He wasn't hot after his snippy offspring. He was hot after me.

The veins in his neck were corded. He growled, "Renney, you're coming, too!"

I stayed on the porch, arms akimbo, and watched his

77

two hundred fifteen pounds plow forward. He stopped at the bottom step and repeated his order.

I said calmly, "I'm not going anywhere, Manie." I leaned forward. "I'm not here to have you tell me what to do."

He waved his meaty hand. "Are you going to get the hell in that car?"

I shook my head and went down one step. I had no choice. If I was supposed to be the boss I had to act like one. If I gave in once I'd be finished.

I said, "Manie, you goddamned ape, if you're worried about that bitchy daughter of yours, forget it!"

He lunged and his fist hammered me on the side of the head. It had little power since I was traveling with the blow. Then the top step caught my heel, I tripped.

I heard Dee scream and other noises. Or did I? I was aware only of Manie's huge frame lunging forward, down on top of me, and rolled desperately. I scrambled to my feet and braced for his next attack.

He swung a roundhouse right and it arched like a boom, missing my jaw by inches. I straightened him with a quick left jab, then crossed with a hard right. He didn't mind me at all. He still came forward, apparently immune to the lefts and rights I caromed off his chin. He just didn't give a damn. His arms were wide, he came on unprotected. He waded in and finally caught and pinned me against a corner of the porch. My knee jabbed for his groin, missed, and his fist dug in low. It was a bomb and it penetrated to my backbone.

I was finished, as quickly as that, and crumpled to the floor, gulping for air. I thought I was going to die.

He didn't follow through. Dee was screaming and hanging on his neck and he tried to flick her off as though she were a pesky mosquito. She must have had a way with him, her cries must have been getting through, because his temper ebbed. He left me and lumbered off the porch.

On the front lawn he walked aimlessly and Dee stayed with him, talking, pleading. She unleashed a ceaseless fire of chatter, aimed to lure him back to sanity. And she did her work well. He stopped his promenade and stood immobile, like a hulking statue, legs apart, head lowered, only his heaving chest indicating that he was alive.

My breath came back and I pulled myself to my feet. I heard Dee say, over and over, "You shouldn't do that, Manie. He's sick!"

He shouldn't do it anyway, sick or not.

I glanced at the car. Tee-hee and Seymour hadn't moved. Tee-hee was grinning, Seymour growling. They hadn't been so dumb, staying where they were. They were smarter than I.

Strength returned and I stumbled off the porch and advanced toward him. Maybe I was crazy. Dee's words echoed in my brain: *When are we going to kill Manie?* It came to me that now was a good time. Mine had become an impulsive hate. None is more dangerous, more violent or more foolish.

I stopped a yard short of him and some little wisp of reason hissed, "Take it easy, boy. Down! Down!"

We glowered at each other and Dee stepped between us. She put both her hands on my chest and pushed. Her eyes were pleading. "Go back to the porch, Apple. Please!"

My words were measured and they meant what they said, "That's not going to happen again, Manie. Ever!"

He didn't move. "Nobody calls my daughter a bitch."

"Please," cried Dee. "Go back."

She knew more about the monster than I did. She got

79

him turned around and headed back to the car. The tires spat gravel, and I watched the Buick vanish through the trees and around a bend in the black, macadam road.

I brushed myself off, glanced around for Carol and Causby, didn't see them, went to the kitchen and doused my face with cool water. My head cleared. My stomach still felt as though I had swallowed an unpeeled pineapple. I hadn't the strength to swear.

Yet, I was lucky. I wasn't in the Buick. I was alone. It was the break I needed and I didn't intend to let it slip by. It was my first chance really to look over the place. Somewhere in this big, wide world Manie had stashed a half million dollars. I wanted to find it. I wanted the reward. Nobody hides that kind of money without a trace. Whether or not the bazooka loot was here, there was a good chance that I might find some indication of its whereabouts in this place.

I tackled the cellar first and I shouldn't have bothered. It held old beer cans, empty cartons and whisky bottles, some rusty tools, several ashcans and a filthy furnace that hadn't been serviced for years. I expected a legion of rodents to scurry out and start gnawing on my legs. None did. Maybe they thought I was crazy.

I retreated upstairs, peeked out of several windows for a glimpse of Causby or Carol, and beat it to the attic. I figured on taking care of the extremes first. If I got nabbed, it would be easier to explain my presence in the livable part of the house.

The attic hadn't been used recently and I was sure that no one had bothered to enter it for a long time. This was evident, because the thick, gray dust on the floor hadn't been disturbed. I didn't disturb it, either. From the top of the stairs I stared at another sloppy scene—boxes, battered suitcases, odd pieces of furniture, one bedpan and, dominating all else, an oversize dressmaker's mannikin. On the second floor, Manie's and Dee's room was heaped with personality clues. Dee's things were neatly in place. Her closet was immaculate and bulged with exquisite dresses and wraps. Manie's closet looked like a fire sale in a second-hand haberdashery. Half of his suits, and he had plenty, were unpressed and he used the floor as a hamper for his dirty shirts, underwear and socks. On a hook in the back hung an empty shoulder holster.

In the top drawer of his bureau I found the iron that fitted the holster. It was a .38 automatic and next to it were two long, narrow boxes of cartridges. The rest was junk.

In the second drawer I found a small bundle of letters squeezed firmly together by a strong rubber band. I slipped off the band, feeling greedy. I pored over every word in every epistle and, while most of them could have been in a foreign language, there was one that rewarded both my curiosity and patience. It was to Manie from Patty Sears.

Patty had written not two weeks ago, ". . . I still can't figure out why Apple wants to leave that deal he's got on the Coast, but he seems real eager. Maybe you can ask him or maybe he'll just tell you himself . . ."

If Manie had no suspicions about Apple's decision to team up with him, he certainly had plenty after that letter, and the information was worth having. Good old Patty, I thought. Sure, I'd tell Manie. I'd just leave off the part about killing him.

I returned the letters to the drawer exactly as I had found them and prepared to wiggle out of there. I didn't, not yet. On the wall was a girly calendar and this I had to look at. Miss August looked exactly like Agnes. Well, her hair was a lighter color and the eyes were smaller, but the rest of her . . . I found myself wondering what Agnes was doing at this moment and if she was still mad at me. I also wondered how many private investigators succeed when they pull their first bank job. No figures came to mind, only the curvacious figure of Miss August who actually seemed to move and dance in front of my eyes.

I think my reverie lasted too long. I know it did, because I was jolted back to reality when I heard, "Find what you were looking for, Mr. Renney?"

I spun around, more angry with myself than anything, and standing in the doorway was Carol. She was smiling like a Mata Hari.

11

IF I DON'T like them, I call them claws, male or female, and Carol was one. But even with Agnes there on the wall, she made a pretty bundle. She leaned against the door, one slim leg crossed over the other, one hand on her hip. She must have been on her way for a swim somewhere, I thought, because she wore a white terry-cloth beach robe. It fell inches short of her knees, a belt pinched it tight to her small waist and the fluffy collar was all mixed up in her long, yellow hair.

At the moment I wasn't too perturbed at the interruption. I had no real idea of the etiquette governing the behavior of one thief in the household of another, but I sensed Carol wasn't too surprised to find me here.

"Hi," I said. "Going swimming?"

She smiled coldly. "You haven't answered me, Mr. Renney."

"That's because you made it a silly question. What makes you think I'm looking for something? Perhaps the door was open and I just wandered in. I've been admiring that calendar on the wall."

She shook her head. "It won't do. You see, I've been in the bathroom—" she jerked her head at an open door— "and I saw you. You seemed to be looking for something."

SO LOVELY TO KILL

When you're caught irrevocably, nothing beats a stout denial. I smiled. "Nothing."

Slowly, deliberately, she withdrew a pack of cigarettes from a pocket in the robe and offered me one. I accepted it, lit hers and mine and took a deep drag, blowing the blue smoke over her head. Ironically, it formed a halo.

She said in mock surprise, "A cigarette? Should you, really, Mr. Renney, so soon after getting over pneumonia."

"I'm coming along," I said, and wanted at that moment, more than anything, to fan her backside. Only the feeling that we both shared a dislike of Manie stopped me.

"I'll say you are," she said. "And this morning? Goodness, the way you swung your fists." She took a drag. "Poor daddy."

"A minor misunderstanding," I said.

"Almost manslaughter, Mr. Renney, except that neither of you carried it far enough."

She stepped into the room and faked a duplication of my search, humming as she did it.

She said throatily, "And in the attic, Mr. Renney, and in the cellar? Did you find what you were looking for there?"

I shrugged. "I was looking for nothing. I found nothing. I'm not in the most secure profession in the world. I always like to check my surroundings."

She didn't reply, dipped her head, signifying the end of our conversation, spun from the room and strode down the hallway to the stairs. I remained for only a second, then took off after her. She hadn't carried it far enough.

"Carol!" I called.

I caught her downstairs at the front door and put my hand on it so she couldn't open it. "Look," I said earnestly,

84

SO LOVELY TO KILL

"so I was snooping around. I told you why. But I don't want Manie to know."

"Why not, if you were just checking?"

"Well, you know Manie."

"Do I, Mr. Renney?" She was chilling me with her smile.

"You should. You're his daughter."

"Aren't I the lucky girl." She said it, but she didn't mean it.

I opened the door for her. What was the use?

Still, she managed to satisfy me. Brushing past, she said, "You won't have to worry about my telling Manie anything. The less I have to do with him, the better I like it."

She didn't turn back. She descended the porch steps, swung around to the back of the house and her walk was as stately and haughty as that of a Kentucky thoroughbred.

The next thing on the agenda was to find Causby and see if he could, or would, tell me anything about his guests I didn't already know. As I set out to find him, I tried to shape such information as I already had into a pattern for the future.

The most menacing problem I had was Dee's early determination to kill Manie, and there were aspects to her eagerness that needed explanation. I could understand why Dee was bent on exterminating her husband —he was brutal and she was in love with another man— but I couldn't understand why she would do it and sacrifice the bazooka money. Eventually, the loot would cool off and bring a tidy profit. Unless—sure! She also knew where the money was. Then, I thought, *God, maybe Carol does, too.* And Causby? Was he in on it?

I moved a little faster, hunting him.

He was in the orchard and I finally knew what his

farm grew. The realization rushed over me like the vapors of a stink bomb. Apples! So help me, Apples! The russet image of one was etched on my body, a symbol of everything that had happened to me since that day at the morgue—and here was this dirty old man growing them!

Causby was standing on a small stepladder and, with a chisel and wooden mallet, was chipping rotten wood out of the trunk of one of his many trees. He saw me approach, relaxed to a sitting position on the top of the ladder, and greeted me sourly. I did not think he wanted to talk. Probably, he was just tired of hacking away.

"Hi," I said cordially. "Why don't you get a tree surgeon to do that?"

He waved the chisel. "I can do it just as good and a darned sight cheaper." He pursed his wrinkled lips and again swung the chisel in an arc, indicating the trees that stretched for acres and acres toward the interior of his farm. "I did them—the ones that needed—and as good as any tree surgeon."

He must have been right about his skill. Most of the trees were thriving and getting ready to yield luscious fruit.

Causby said, "I used to get a tree surgeon till Manie taught me how."

I was surprised. "Manie."

"Sure," he said, and shifted on his perch and I thought he'd fall. But he was agile and held his balance. "He knows a lot for a city fellow. Does plenty of putterin' around when he has the time. He fixed my truck and redone that room in the barn for that daughter of his, and he even dug me an irrigation ditch on the south side of the orchard."

"He's quite a guy," I said.

He agreed. "Sure. I bet he did ten or a dozen trees

86

hisself till I learnt it. You just chisel out the bad wood and fill the holes up with that there black cement. That's about all there is to it."

There was one tree that hadn't fared as well as the others, I noted. Many of the branches were dead, though the tree still bore some small, pink-green apples. He saw me looking at it and was prompted to apologize. "Course, you can't save them all. That one Manie and me did together, but it was diseased too far through. Sap can't run no more."

"Why don't you cut it down?"

He nodded. "Will one of these days."

"Manie been here long?" I asked.

"Oh, sure. Off and on for two years about—ever since that there bazooka trial. I guess it's two years."

"What do you mean, off and on?" I asked.

He faced me and let me concentrate on his sick, white eye. "Suppose you ask Manie that, young fella."

I told him I would and he added brusquely, "I don't ask no questions. I don't answer none about my guests. Not even you."

Most elderly persons you try to like despite their idiosyncrasies, but Causby, I couldn't. I doubted further friendliness would buy me anything, so I left him, wondering if he was a wise old rat or just a damned fool.

I turned to the back of the farm, cut through a corner of the orchard to a road that led into the dense woodland. I had paced off less than a hundred yards when the old guy called after me and there was urgency in his tone. "Hey! You'd better not go down to the river. That Carol's down there."

His inflection indicated that he didn't think much of the snip, either. I called back, "So?"

"Well, you know Manie. He don't like stuff like that."

87

SO LOVELY TO KILL

I nodded and said I'd stay away from her, wheeled around and continued on my way. Where to? To Carol, who evidently had gone swimming after all. Nothing could happen if she didn't see me.

The dirt road I traveled narrowed as it plunged past the orchard and into the forest. Away from the house, away from Causby, and answerable to no one, the world took on beauty. The warm, golden rays of the sun, the purring breeze and the multi-shaded greens of trees and bushes and ferns, the petals of sprightly flowers frolicked together and produced a thrilling, mobile design. Above, the sky was a pure pastel blue and it was tufted near the horizon with mounds of white clouds. I felt free and strode aimlessly.

After a quarter mile or more, the road narrowed sharply and become nothing more than a foot path. It remained well used however.

I reached the river and got a laugh out of Causby's imagination. His river was a creek and the water flashed white as it broke over protruding rocks.

I proceeded along the bank. At one point the path skirted back from the stream, bypassing an obstructing clay knoll, and in behind the knoll I stopped and frowned. There was a small clearing and in the middle were two neat gravestones. The earth around them was immaculately groomed and amber and yellow flowers swayed peacefully in the mild summer breeze. I hadn't the faintest idea what the flowers were, but they were pretty and silently devout. One stone was inscribed to the memory of Mildred Causby, dead for twenty years according to the legend. The other grave belonged to Causby's son, who, apparently, never reached adulthood, since he had been dead for over forty years. The neatness of the plots impressed me and I was compelled to revamp my opinion

SO LOVELY TO KILL

of Causby. He had some sentiment after all.

Breaking the silence came a splash, the familiar sound of a body meeting water. I moved past the miniature cemetery back to the path. I stopped high above the stream, where the bank was steep, rutted with erosion canals caused by the rush of rain water. Fifty yards down, the water widened, forming a sizable pool, protected by a wall and canopy of green vegetation. The water shivered with silver ripples, patched here and there with the reflection of the blue sky. The spot was peaceful, beautiful and strangely private—I felt almost like a trespasser.

And then I did feel like an intruder.

Carol was in the pool. Slowly, effortless she swam across it. Her yellow bathing cap bobbed like a ball and her slim, golden arms sliced through the water with flawless, rhythmical grace. Halfway across she rolled over on her back and floated, now and again fluttering her feet, splashing diamonds of water into the air. She made a picture of loveliness here, as she had not done at the house, and I wondered at her earlier malice and bitterness. Yet, I shouldn't have. She was Manie's daughter. He could ruin the best in the world.

Presently, she stood and I realized that the water was shallow. It barely covered her hips. She wore a one-piece bathing suit and stood motionless, her head down, arms folded across her breasts, lost in meditation, about what I'll never know.

I continued to gaze, only mildly aware that I was intruding on her private moment, then silently trod over to a log and sat down.

This I shouldn't have done—there was a nervous buzzing. The motion was too quick to be detected by the naked eye, but the portent was there and I didn't

89

waste time thinking about it. I hopped off the log and started to sprint.

I felt dagger stings on my back, through my shirt and thin sweater, as I taxied down the bank and took off like a B-36, shouting the warning to Carol as I flew.

I knifed into the cool water and my stomach bounced on the gooey bottom. Slime billowed over me and it was a foul sensation—like being thrown into a barrel of eels. I gave a frog kick and, remaining under water, stroked to the center of the pool. I stayed under until my lungs could take it no longer, then emerged cautiously. I stood, finally, soaked and bedraggled, my back and arms smarting from the stings.

Carol's head popped out of the water and, after reconnoitering the area, she stood, too, and immediately her face lost its severe mien. She laughed merrily, pointing her finger at me.

"You looked so funny," she said. "I thought you'd lost your mind."

I sank into the water, washed off the mud, then waded to shore, looking and feeling like a dope. She followed me and her glee didn't subside. This part was amazing. I hadn't thought she was capable of so much laughter.

I peeled off my sweater. Carol stopped laughing, though a merry smirk was on her lips and her eyes were twinkling.

She said, "Gosh, did you move fast."

"I had no choice. I had to."

She chuckled again, threw her head back and closed her eyes. She seemed so childlike, so utterly different, that I ogled her just to make sure she was the same girl.

She shed her bathing cap, letting her honey hair cascade to her shoulders and I took off my shirt and undershirt. The pain was getting worse.

SO LOVELY TO KILL

"Did they get you?" she asked.

"A few of them."

"Let's see."

I turned around and she inspected my back. "A little mud will help.'

She bent down for her towel and, in doing so, the top of her one-piece bathing suit sagged. At first I thought it was an accident. I knew otherwise when she straightened, and she did nothing to pull the suit back into place. I didn't stir and she didn't move, didn't flinch, didn't mind at all, and her eyes burned into mine.

I won the silent battle. She moved, ending that eternity. stood, came around and started to dry my arms and back.

"I'll do that," I said. A tingling sensation spread over my skin when she rested her hot hand on the small of my back. I was hoping, strangely, that she'd continue and that's exactly what she did without saying a word.

Presently she scooped some mud from the river bank and began to dot my arms and back where the bees had stabbed me. It felt cool. She had a sure, gentle touch and I was almost glad I had disturbed the hive. I felt on the verge of a discovery.

"You're in pretty good shape to do all that running after your pneumonia."

I faced her, her first aid finished, and asked, "Why all these cracks about my pneumonia? Am I supposed to be in a wheel chair?"

She cocked her head, appearing not like Carol at all. "I'm merely impressed," she said softly.

"I take good care of myself."

"I bet you do."

She spread the towel on the ground and lay down on it. She said, "So you found my little retreat, Mr. Renney?"

91

I glanced around, still able to appreciate it. "It's nice," I said. "Very nice."

She lit a cigarette, didn't offer me one, and blew the smoke in my direction. She put one arm behind her head for support and her tanned legs parted. Her movements seemed natural enough, not necessarily purposely trying to arouse me, but they had the same effect.

I didn't move. Maybe Renney would have. But there was an honesty about this spot—and suddenly I was Johnny Fury. Afraid of brazen girls.

She said, "You'd better not tell Manie you saw me here. You know him well enough by this time to know what he'd do."

I readily agreed. "I don't intend to."

She seemed to be musing. Her voice had a far off quality as though she were talking to herself or dreaming. "He doesn't know as much as he thinks he does. He doesn't know, for example, that I despise him."

I didn't reply. I liked what she was saying.

"And Dee," she said. "She isn't quite as wise as she thinks she is, either."

"About what?"

She tilted her head and her hair shifted on her shoulders. "Oh, about you, for example.'

Now I didn't like what she was saying. "What about me?"

"Oh, nothing. Nothing of importance. Besides, I don't understand you yet. It's much too soon."

"I had assumed that you understood me fairly well."

She didn't reply, not to that. As though I hadn't spoken, she said, "I come down here at night sometimes when they go to bed and when it's hot. Sometimes the mosquitoes aren't bad and a dip feels good."

"Every night?"

"Every hot night," she emphasized. "For example, tonight it probably will be hot."

She tossed and I caught it. "That sounds like an invitation."

"It isn't, Mr. Renney." She dropped her eyes. "But the water is free."

"I like free things."

"I bet you do. In this case, I'm referring only to the water."

I got the feeling that she was about to manufacture ice again, so I didn't hang around. I gathered my clothes and left her, not saying thanks, not saying anything.

Frankly, I was confused. But I felt I was about to make a friend. One way or another.

12

PASSING THE ORCHARD on the way back, I noted that
Causby had taken my advice. He had lugged a hand
power saw out to the one dead tree and, at that moment,
was stringing an electric extension from the first floor
of the barn.

He looked in my direction as I sloshed along. He said
nothing. Perhaps with his poor eyesight he didn't even
see me.

Quickly I got into dry clothes, returned to the first
floor. Causby was still in the orchard. Then I saw Carol.
She strolled leisurely back from the brook, swinging her
towel, and entered the barn.

It came to me that I had something to tell Matt Nugent,
and that it might be a long time before another opportunity offered. I wasted no time getting on the kitchen
phone. From here I could watch the main entrance to the
house and guard against interruption.

In a matter of seconds laughing boy was throbbing on
the other end.

"Lieutenant Matthew Nugent," he chirped.

"Hi," I said softly, "this is your masquerading McIn-
tosh."

"Huh?"

"The apple on the stick."

SO LOVELY TO KILL

There was a pregnant pause, a vacuum that stretched from Ogsinto to Manhattan Island. Then came the dawn.

"Johnny! For God's sake."

"No names, please," I cautioned. "This is a party line, understand?"

"Yeah, sure, sure. Everything okay?"

"Sugar dandy—and just about as sticky."

"Explain."

"Hold on to your hat—I'm going to pitch curves. You remember the apple used to be afraid of being run over by a grass train with a lovely caboose?"

He took a little time to let that sink in. Then he said, "Yeah—I think I get it."

"Well, the apple's been living in the caboose for a long, long time. They liked it that way."

Matt emitted a low whistle. Then he asked softly, "How's the apple now?"

"So far," I said, "he's still the apple of her eye. I guess we can chalk it up to luck, love, the night and an apparent similarity in techniques."

He said, "My God!"

I purred softly, "This part I hate."

"I bet!"

"I mean it, and it's getting worse. There's another little caboose on a side track. I don't know how long I can keep her there. I'm going to meet her at the round-house tonight."

"What roundhouse?"

"Oh, just a little spot where hot choo-choos meet to blow off steam."

"Damn it all!" Matt shouted. "I didn't send you up there to indulge in your damned vices—"

"Take it easy, Matt. This little caboose just might like to break up the train."

That quieted him. After a while he asked, "Anything else?"

"Yeah—the first caboose has been planning to feed the train a poisoned apple."

"Oh, my God!" Matt sounded genuinely concerned. "Watch your step up there, will you? Listen, if you get into something you can't handle, I've alerted the people in Winslow—"

I swore softly under my breath, while Matt went on about the fine cooperation between big city cops and smalltown flatfeet. If the police at Winslow had been alerted, with Manie's suspicious nature, there could be some fine complications just ahead. But before I could say anything to Matt, I heard Causby thumping up the back porch steps.

I hung up, scooped my wet clothes up from the kitchen floor, swung toward the door and was well on my way out when he saw me. He couldn't, I thought, possibly suspect a thing. We slid past one another and, with all the decorum of rattlesnakes, said nothing. I don't think he noticed my wet clothes.

He saw me hanging them up to dry when he returned from the house, carrying a long screwdriver. He made no comment, but I had a hunch that plenty was racing through his mind.

Draping the clothes over the line, I said, "Decided to cut it down anyway, eh?"

"Yep." He nodded. "Might as well." He seemed to be thinking something over carefully. Finally he said, "Yep," again, and trudged back to the orchard. Manie, I thought, would get a full report on my wet clothes.

That was it for the day. I sat on the porch and waited for Manie. The day was calm, hot—I remember staring at a mountain in the distance and wondering if there was a breeze on the other side.

When Manie, Dee and the Marchettis finally got back, the heat of the day became one of my lesser problems. The big thing for everybody became Manie's temper. Either he hadn't gotten over our morning scrap, or something had happened in town to bother him. He roamed from room to room, restlessly, growling at Dee, the Marchettis, at Carol, and finally at me.

Eventually I got him calmed down enough to get some idea of what had been going on in town. The Marchettis' story was about what I'd expected—they'd neither seen nor heard anything useful—actually my reason for sending them had been to establish a precedent in their brutish minds for taking orders from me. When, and if, things really began to rock along, any divided loyalty on the part of the brothers could be useful.

That I'd already made some headway was suggested by Seymour's growling reaction when Manie muttered something about: ". . . gotta change the goddam plans . . ."

"Plans?" he said. "What we need plans for? We walk in, we walk out—just take care of the cop."

Manie swore. "Cop? where the hell were you looking? Sure there was a cop. But what about them state troopers hanging around?"

That was the first I'd heard of state troopers, and I thought of Matt Nugent's alerting the local cops. It was working out just about as I had feared—he had also alerted Manie.

None of this bothered the brothers Marchetti.

Seymour growled, "So it was just one of those days. State cops move around."

Manie was not convinced. He was looking at me. He said, "I hope to God you're right."

97

SO LOVELY TO KILL

I said, "What's wrong, Manie? You think I'm a cop, too?"

That earned a giggle from Tee-hee, and Seymour gave me what for him would pass for a thoughtful look. Manie glared at everybody.

I said quickly, "You're right, though, Manie—we've got to find the reason for any extra cops. In the meantime, there're other things to work out. Let's get started."

We spent the rest of the day poring over maps, time schedules, figuring out alternate escape routes, signals and emergency changes in plans in case anything went wrong. We even rehearsed the actual holdup and the various foreseeable exigencies.

By the time we knocked off, the Marchettis were a subdued pair, and there was a grudging respect in Manie's eyes. I was not surprised—I had been a little carried away myself. For a private eye, I was beginning to think I would make a hell of a good bank robber.

It was decided I would try to spot the bank's alarm system, the next day. I anticipated no trouble. I knew alarm systems inside and out—had supervised the installation of enough of them. What I didn't like were lobsters and guns and bullets and things.

After supper I volunteered to help Dee with the dishes, and the members of the small, illustrious household scattered like buckshot in a variety of directions. All, that is, except Manie who lazily, but wisely, remained in the living room, within earshot.

I had intended to pump Dee. After all, we were an alliance—hon and dearie—and if she wouldn't confide in a potential fellow murderer, whom would she confide in? But the opportunity didn't come until Causby hobbled along and convinced Manie that he should look at a tree in the west end of the orchard which he thought needed attention. Manie was reluctant at first, but finally trudged away with the old man.

Dee did not delay when she knew we were alone. Her arms coiled around my waist. Her lips reached for mine and her hips began to churn.

I got her off it. "Baby, after the bank job. I have it all figured."

"Oh, Apple, good," she said.

"But you gotta help."

"Honey, I'll help, you know that."

She squeezed me enthusiastically.

I said carefully, holding her tightly and trying to keep my mind where it belonged. "I'll kill Manie all right and you won't have to worry, but there's something else we've got to work out. After all, I'm sticking my neck out."

At that second I was stretching my neck out a rural mile.

She nestled her head on my chest. "What are you talking about?"

I gave it to her, right between her bedroom eyes. "The bazooka money. How are we going to handle it?"

Well, I had said it, as ambiguously as I could—now I waited to see if the room would explode.

It didn't. For a moment nothing happened. Then she stirred and purred softly, "Don't you trust me, honey?"

That was all she said and that was all she had to say. She knew where the bazooka loot was, and Apple didn't. It figured—she wouldn't have missed a hold like that over her paramour. From here I could push it all the way home.

"Sure I trust you," I said in a whisper, "but I have to know."

She raised her face to mine. She was relaxed and her eyes were moist and tender. "You promised me, Apple.

99

You promised. You agreed we'd forget it until we've killed Manie."

"Yeah, yeah," I said. "But I've been thinking—"

This time her retort was firm. "After we kill Manie!"

That ended it. A lusty monotone, the strains of *"Yes, sir, that's my baby . . ."* told us that Manie was returning from the orchard.

I didn't care. I was glad to shake Dee loose.

13

MANIE THREW ME a suspicious look as he came in, and I could figure out why. He had been talking to Causby. But it wasn't until a little before eleven that Manie got around to asking me. It must have taken all the patience he owned for him to remain quiet so long, but with bedtime creeping up on us, he could restrain himself no longer.

He said quietly, out of nowhere, "Renney—how come you got all wet?"

"I jumped in the river," I shot back.

"Why?"

"I sat on some bees."

He looked at me as though I were crazy. Manie was sitting on the sofa and Dee was curled up next to him, her fingers playing with the nape of his neck. She was making a big show of marital affection.

Causby wasn't there, having retired to his kitchen bunk early as usual. Carol read her magazine and the Marchettis, sitting at a table in the front of the living room, cursed and griped their way through a gin rummy game. All of us were drinking beer.

"Why'd you go down to the river?" Manie asked.

I gave him the same pitch I'd given Carol earlier in Manie's room. "I could ask what the hell it's to you, Manie—but I'll tell you. I like to know the lay of the land wherever I'm holed up. I was just looking the place over."

"See Carol?"

The girl didn't look up.

I said disgustedely, "Hell, no, Manie."

Seymour twisted his skinny body around and rasped, "Smart guy Renney, huh? Bees!"

His sleepy-eyed brother read into Seymour's words a fabulous humor. "Tee-hee," he snickered. "Wise guy—big deal."

Okay, I thought. If we were going to play games I had more to contribute to the waning evening that the rest of them. At least I had the big question.

So I popped it and it sent the lid flying off the night.

I said, "Manie, I got a deal."

"Huh?"

"A deal." I paused. "I'm in a position to give you sixty cents on the dollar for the bazooka money."

There was no lull; the action began at once. Dee's hand had been poised next to Manie's cheek. Now her fingernails dug into the soft, bruised flesh where I had slugged him earlier.

Manie let out a yell, knocked Dee's arm away and planted a vicious slap across her mouth. Dee stood up, her face tight.

"What the hell are you doing?"

"I told you not to touch my cheek," he bellowed.

Manie growled something unintelligible, and she went for him, her fists striking at his bulk in futile, feminine fury. Manie took it for perhaps five seconds; then he locked her wrists in one big paw, drew his free arm back and struck her with his closed fist. Her head bounced against the back of the sofa and she was instantly silent, stunned.

102

SO LOVELY TO KILL

I started to get up, thought better of it, and pushed back into my chair, tense and ready. Apparently I was the only one concerned.

Carol flipped a page.

Tee-hee cried, "Gin!"

Seymour answered, "Marone!"

Dee was coming to. Slowly, sullenly, she began to call Manie names. She had little originality but a lot of venom—each low-spoken word came out with savage, spitting impact.

Manie swung again. Her head snapped back. Then, as though jolted with electricity, she wrested free from his grasp, bolted from the sofa and stood over him. Her fists were tight, her knuckles white, her whole body was shaking.

She yelled hysterical obscenities.

"Shut up, you slut," Manie said mildly.

He made a move for her and she retreated, having had enough. She turned her back to him. The final signal of surrender came when she buried her face in her hands and began to sob.

No one said anything. Carol flipped the pages of her magazine. Seymour and Tee-hee kept playing—the slap of their cards helped to measure time. It seemed longer than it actually was before Dee stopped crying. She straightened her wide shoulders and took up a position behind the couch, where Manie couldn't see her.

She glared at me, and I couldn't blame her.

Manie took a gulp of beer. He seemed undisturbed by the recent commotion. He looked at me and said, "What was that you were talking about a minute ago? A deal?"

"I offered you sixty cents on the dollar for the bazooka dough."

103

SO LOVELY TO KILL

He didn't jump and start pounding me on the back. I might have said, "It looks like rain," for all the interest he showed. He stared at me, his enigmatic face screwed up in that too-friendly, yet dangerous smile.

I said, "Don't be a horse's neck, Manie. You know me well enough, at least by reputation, to go along with me. There's nothing harebrain about this—it'll be a legitimate exchange."

Still, he said nothing. He gulped more beer, used his wrist for a napkin and rolled his shoulders—a motion I had come to regard as a sign of positive thinking on his part. I watched him. Manie versus the mind.

At last he said slowly, "So that's what this little deal was leading to."

I shrugged. "All deals lead to something. I thought you might have guessed."

"I didn't!" he shot back. The thought seemed to disturb him. "I never tumbled. I just wondered why you wanted in with me. You had a good deal on the Coast. They wondered—" he nodded over his shoulder at the Marchettis—"Patty Sears wondered."

"I know he did," I said. "I figured it was none of his business."

"And the bank job, Renney? We still going ahead on that?"

"Sure," I told him. "That's still on. I'd just as soon kill two birds. I figured you'd think the same way."

Manie was nodding slowly. Dee looked frightened now. Carol still didn't seem to care.

"Sure," Manie said. "I'd go for a deal like that. But I got news for you, Apple—there ain't no bazooka dough. Maybe you don't read the papers too well. Seymour, Tee-hee and me got acquitted for that job, remember?

SO LOVELY TO KILL

Mistaken identity or something. No dough, no deal, no nothing."

"Crabs," I said, and leaned forward in my chair. "I'm giving you a chance to get out from under. You won't get sixty per cent any place else. You know who I am, so why act so innocent. You'll get a fair shake and a guarantee of protection."

Manie Grass slid forward, too, and Dee closed her eyes in exasperation. I didn't worry about it. I could take care of her later. I knew it now.

"Who sent you here, Renney?"

"I sent myself," I said.

Seymour got interested. He moved forward and stood next to Dee. "You can fence a half million bucks all by yourself, Renney? You're real smart."

Tee-hee lived up to his name, as he moved forward, too. "You must be real smart."

"Well, forget it," interrupted Manie. He waved his hand for silence and obediently it fell. "There ain't no bazooka dough. It's the God's honest truth, Apple."

"Maybe you'll warm up as I go along," I said.

He hunched his shoulders and grinned that paternal warm, friendly grin. "There aint a fire hot enough. But out of curiosity—"

"Yeah," said Seymour, his dark face pinched. "How'd you figure to fence that much dough?"

I exposed my palms. "I have the contact. One contact. Who it is is none of your business. All you have to know is that the dough you'll get in exchange will be good." I took a cigarette, fired it, watching my hand shake slightly, and admitted generously, "As for the rest, it will be fenced through every bookie in L.A., on a Saturday. All winnings on horses and numbers will be paid off with the bazooka money. By Monday morning it should be spread all over California."

"You mean," said Manie, "one big outlay? Boom! Like that!"

"Like that."

He laughed and it was a low, raucous rumbling. "And what happens when they trace it to the books?"

"Let them trace it," I said. "How long can they keep a couple of thousand books in jail?"

"And then they start to talk."

"Let them talk. They can't say a helluva lot if they don't know where the money came from."

Manie toasted me with the beer can. "Brave man."

"Smart man," said Seymour, "or maybe dumb man. How can you do such a thing—get books to hand out hot dough and nobody knows where it came from?"

"That's also my business," I said.

"Awful brave," said Manie and his big, beefy head bobbed back and forth. He finished his beer and tossed the empty can to the end of the couch. "You don't mind making people mad, do you, Renney?"

There was a strained silence and I knew they were thinking it over. Dee's eyes were still closed and she didn't look attractive any more—she looked old. Her black hair was disarranged, her eyelids were red and her cheeks were puffed like putty. For her it was a dreadful interlude, waiting for Manie to reply.

She got the answer she wanted. Manie said, "I sure wish I had that money." His utterance had all the reverence of a prayer.

"You'll think it over, Manie?" I asked.

He spread his lips thin. "I'll dream."

That finished it, at least for the time being. Carol distracted attention from me when she scaled her maga-

SO LOVELY TO KILL

zine over to the sofa. It landed on top of Manie's beer can.

She stood up and said, "I'm going to bed." To her father she murmured, "I'd stay around if I thought there'd be another floor show."

He was preoccupied and let the remark pass.

"Or, maybe, Daddy dear, you'd like to slap me around for a while."

"Shut up and beat it," he growled.

Her young, round hips rolled enticingly as she passed. I watched, but made believe I didn't. She said to no one in particular, "It's hot as hell," and was gone.

It was her second invitation. Still, she couldn't possibly have known how appropriate her remark was. It was hell hot—I almost felt my body char as I encountered the intense eyes of Manie, Dee and the celebrated morons.

14

MATT'S TIDY little plan had drawn a big zero. *Manie'll jump at it,* Matt had said. Sure, he jumped all right—almost as far as a dead dinosaur. Of course, with Manie, all this could be pure caution. After all, the dough was hot, and he couldn't rush into things. But maybe I could now highpressure Dee into faster action—a lot depended on how deeply she loved Apple Renney.

Back in my room, I waited before switching on the light. Sitting next to the window, I peered through the night at the barn. I could see little. No light showed in the barn and I could spot no movement in the indigo-yellow infusion of moonlight.

Around me were the small sounds the rest of the menagerie made bedding down. I waited, not for final peace, but for Dee. She would risk seeing me tonight, I knew. She would have to. She would want to know why I had popped after we, supposedly, had everything planned.

I lit a cigarette and kept the ashes short so that the glow might be seen. If Carol saw it, she would know I was biding my time. *Soon, kid, soon. . . . You're next on the bazooka parade.*

Carol! I filled my mind with her and tried to understand. Either she was a nice kid with a potentially warm

SO LOVELY TO KILL

personality or she was a two-faced bitch. At the river, this
morning, she had been human. During the evening she
had been wound up again—I had sensed her readiness
to explode at any point, at any or all of us. That included
me. Then why request my attendance at a nocturnal hide-
away, another way of saying to any normal male that we
should sneak behind the bushes? I shrugged in the darkness and smoked the butt down to my fingers, waiting to
find out.

Dee eased the door open, as I had guessed she would,
and slipped noiselessly into the room. Tonight she was
in the grip of another kind of passion. Her face was
taut with anger and she took off on me with a severity
that spoke only of distrust. She was only slightly ham-
pered by having to whisper. I was not merely a bungling
male. I was a turncoat—a scurvy son of a slobby old thing
who had decided to cheat.

She was in a white, gossamer nightgown that didn't
weaken any of her arguments. Even in the dim light,
it was easy to see she was all there. Not one limb nor
appendage was AWOL and the twin badges of her sex
stood high and proud, liquid in motion, and pointing as
dogmatically and eagerly as two young hitch-hikers.

I grabbed her by the shoulders, said nothing and felt
deliriously self-confident. It seemed only right that I
should turn on a little heat of my own.

"Baby!" I breathed, and my hands began to roam. She
didn't stop me and neither did she respond.

"Apple!" her tongue was lashing, quietly caustic.

"Shut up," I said, and kissed her.

"Apple!"

"Huh?"

"Are you on your own now, you idiot? Is that the
deal?"

109

"What are you babbling about?" I replied, inferring that her anger was groundless. I vised my arms around her and for a minute we said nothing. She was still waiting, though. I tilted her chin up. "Look, baby, don't call me an idiot. I know what I'm doing. I had to tell him something. He's suspicious and I had to give him some reason for my being here. Even a moron would know that a two-bit bank deal wouldn't pull me away from my setup on the Coast. Nor would a chance to tie in with a musclehead like Manie."

"But why a fence? Why put that in his head?"

"I had to make it strong, so he'd believe me. Besides, I could really do it that way. I've got the man to work it."

"I told you I had the fence."

I took a chance, a big one, basing my odds on how worried she'd seemed earlier.

I said, "Not for sixty per cent, baby."

The chance paid off. "Fifty's all right." Her head was on my shoulder. "It's all we need."

I felt an absurd elation which, as those things will, translated itself into the form of self-expression closest to hand. The squeeze I gave Dee must have carried extra conviction, because she came against me like a soft cloud.

"Baby," I said. "If I can make us sixty, we'll make sixty. Besides, there's one little thing about us that always bothered me—you never trusted me about that money. I'm not saying you'd double-cross me with Manie, but I feel better now that you know you couldn't get anywhere with him with your lousy fifty per cent."

She didn't resent it—this was her language. Her mind was like water; it sought its lowest level. Wallowing there, she became pacified, and I could see why she and Apple had hit it off so well.

She nuzzled me and whispered, without resentment,

110

SO LOVELY TO KILL

"I love you, honey, and we'll get the money together, after he's dead. What ever per cent you decide." Then she added, her voice rife with conjecture: "But I'm not so sure any more."

"About what?"

"About the money. I know it's here, because I was with him when he brought it and I thought I knew where he'd hidden it, but now I'm not so sure."

It was my turn to be angry and, believe me, I wasn't faking.

"You told me you knew!"

"Well, I thought I knew."

"It's a damn big farm. You could plow up a hundred acres for the next hundred years and still not find it."

"I think I know, Apple. I'm almost sure."

"Well, where, then?"

She chuckled, kissed me on the neck, and moaned affectionately, "After we kill Manie."

That again. "And the Marchettis?" I asked. It occurred to me that something would have to happen to them, too. "And Causby?"

She said almost sleepily, "Manie and I will take care of them."

She looked at me. Her eyes were moist and blazing. She opened her mouth and ran her tougue over her white teeth. She breathed heavily, as though driven by an unworldly hunger, deep-rooted ecstasies that ignored danger and made a piker of desire. And then it came to me—she loved death. Kill Manie. Kill the Marchettis. Kill Causby. Kill Carol? Kill her, too?

I couldn't ask. It wasn't in me.

My arms tightened around her and I couldn't see her expression. I didn't want to. I couldn't trust my face not to betray the nausea that was churning within me.

111

SO LOVELY TO KILL

"When you let Manie have it—you'll let me watch? I have to be sure?"

"Yes, you can watch."

She shivered. "I ought to see it—after what he's done to my life. Kiss me, honey."

I did.

Dee slipped out of the room, out of sight, not quite out of mind.

Minutes became eons, then, as I waited for slumber to overtake the members of the household. The wait was eternal. I lay on the bed with my clothes on, watching deep shadows and streaks of reflected moonlight wiggle on the ceiling.

I heard one snore, then two and I would have given odds that they belonged to the Marchettis. One actually seemed a growl. The other was a juvenile gurgle, high-pitched and grating on the nerves. From what I had seen of Manie, Dee would be enough to hold him oblivious, whatever he was doing to her.

The time was now. I stood and clung close to the wall. Earlier I had found that the floor boards toward the center of the room were swayback and squeaky. Near the baseboard they were reasonably silent. I reached the door, twisted the knob—and didn't open it.

Two dry planks of wood rubbed together and screamed, their raw nerve-grains exposed to each other.

Somebody growled, "Quiet."

A higher-pitched whisper replied, "I can't help it."

I could have laughed.

Dee and Manie were outside, in the hallway, playing the same game as I.

They reached my door, passed it, treading as lightly as

they could. Then I thought of what might have happened, had I started out two seconds earlier, and any amusement I had felt vanished in cold sweat.

I was confused and stood immobile, scarcely breathing, listening. Dee and Manie practically owned the farmhouse—why did they choose to sneak around like a couple of second-story amateurs? It wasn't solely because they didn't wish to awaken anyone. Consideration for others was not one of their outstanding virtues.

There came another squeal and another muffled reprimand and to this one Dee gave no reply. In the filmy darkness I saw the outline of their bodies. When they reached the first floor, they swung toward the kitchen. For all I knew they couldn't sleep and were after a couple of cans of beer. I heard the kitchen door close—and a sense of relief swept over me. I had business of my own tonight.

I closed the door to my room and wedged a wooden match in the crevice. It would tell me later if they had gotten snoopy. I went downstairs, shunned the kitchen and slipped noiselessly out the front door.

Curiosity, in addition to a love for my own hide, prompted me to check on Manie and Dee when I reached the back of the house. The kitchen light was on. It was shrouded by a ribald blue shade and the square window and the black house reminded me of an early century painting. It wasn't ugly. It wasn't pretty. It just was. I edged to the window and stood on my toes. I enjoyed a wide angle of vision.

Causby was sleeping. He was flat on his back and the ceiling light hadn't disturbed him. His breathing was deep and regular. I leaned to the side and saw Manie. Strangely, he was clearing the kitchen table. He transferred the salt and pepper shakers, a napkin rack and a

113

sugar bowl to the cupboard, then he slipped the oil cloth cover off the table and spread it on the floor next to Causby's bunk.

I couldn't see Dee, but, responding to Manie's nod, she broke into view and I saw that she held a long spatula in her right hand.

I was wrong.

And it happened too swiftly for me to react, except inwardly, and then with horror and revulsion. She raised her arm high and, as Manie suddenly clapped his hand over Causby's mouth, Dee's arm plunged down, in her grasp not a spatula. It was a knife and the long, tapered steel speared into the old man's chest. He jolted, as I did, feeling the same shock and pain. His eyes popped open and they remained that way and then he settled back, his head on the pillow and he didn't move. He couldn't. He was dead.

Instantly, I was sick and cold. I beat it around to the side of the house and heaved. I couldn't help myself. Long ago I had learned that death and John Fury didn't go together. Yet what sickened me was not the death alone—it was Dee. She was human garbage, more dangerous, I realized, than Manie. Manie, I felt, would have chanced it to trust old Causby. Not Dee. He was a pitfall and he had to be eliminated.

Well, he had been.

Still, I should have anticipated something like this when she had said, "Manie and I will take care of them—" but anticipation of a vague threat never quite prepares one for the reality. I stood there, shocked, knowing I should have gone into that kitchen and confronted them—feeling I should have done something to stop them. But it had been done so quickly—what could I have done? And what could I accomplish by breaking in on them now?

114

SO LOVELY TO KILL

Causby was dead.

I crouched in the deep shadows, and didn't move. The back door creaked open and Dee and Manie entered the night. She still held the knife, it seemed to me almost lovingly, as though she planned to keep it as a trophy. The two of them carried Causby, wrapped in the oilcloth.

I had already had proof of Dee's physical strength. I almost upchucked again, remembering how she had exerted it on the night of my arrival, and watching her now.

She had one end of the oilcloth bundle, Manie the other. They moved stealthily, skirting the orchard, then broke into a near-trot, heading toward the river. Dee handled her end with consummate ease.

One thing puzzled me. I had assumed that they were planning to bury Causby—yet they carried no shovel. Just a knife, and Manie held an unlighted kerosene lantern.

I followed, clinging close to protective foliage. Unless she had set an elaborate trap for me, Carol was at the river—but I was willing to gamble that none of my current playmates were that complex or subtle. Carol would have played hell trying to explain a plot like that against me to Manie, and Manie himself wouldn't have thought of it in a thousand years.

Manie and Dee came to a halt at the water's edge. I crept closer, using the Braille system on the moist ground and avoiding dry sticks that might snap and betray me. I avoided logs, too. I remembered the bees. My lookout was perfect, behind rambling, wild shrubs and wide-leafed ferns.

Manie lighted the lantern and they began. Began what? I was damned if I knew.

But then I averted my gaze. I knew what they were

115

up to when Dee began to wield the blade.

Within the hour the orgy was over and I had lost faith—lost faith in people, and in myself. Living, that quickly, had become a universal crime. It might be well to skip the details. Causby, what was left to him, was returned to the oil cloth. He was carried to the orchard and there he was cemented in to several of the larger trees.

I remembered the painstaking way he had dug his graves.

PART TWO

. . . Into The Fire

15

MY MIND tried to make a fog of it and it didn't come
off. I couldn't blur. I could do nothing but stand there
clammy and cold, and become aware, occasionally, that
rage was shaking me.

I had crouched at the rim of the orchard and watched
Manie manipulate the trowel, slapping his special cement
into cavities which had been chiseled out not long ago. I
saw him smooth out the surface lovingly, with the pride of
an expert. I watched them return to the river and wash
the oilcloth. Quietly, alert to sound and movement, they
returned the masonry equipment to the barn. The knife
was back in the kitchen drawer, the oilcloth was on the
table. There was no evidence that murder had been com-
mitted. Simply that an old man had disappeared. Their
plan had been cunning and foolproof—except that I had
seen them do it.

Then the frustration which was tormenting me dis-
integrated. *I had seen them do it.* Their chances in front
of a jury were absolutely non-existent. Already they were
dead. It was all over for the rest of us, too. I knew now
where the money was. Where else could it be?

So beat it, I told myself. Head for town. Tell the police.
Telephone Matt Nugent. It was all over. Plenty of people
had lost, but I had won.

SO LOVELY TO KILL

No, not yet. There was still Carol. A cog in the mindless intrigue—or something set apart? *Clear it up, Fury. She's basically decent—maybe. If she isn't, maybe that, too, is something you ought to know . . .*

Though the moon had begun its descent in the star-glittering summer sky, I could see well enough to trot instead of walk along the road that led to the river. I felt ill all over again when I passed the site of the butchery, a scenic nook in nature's opulent design. My stomach pained, my head was feverish and light.

I reached the two tombstones, pallid and cold, circled them and descended into Carol's pool.

She was in the water, a jewel amidst jewels, a creature warm and alive in what should have been a rural basin of cool, clear water. But it was red water now. Sad water.

She saw me as I moved up to the bank and, standing, she cocked her head and smiled. "Hi! I thought you'd forgotten."

"Get out of the water," I said gruffly, "it's dirty."

She laughed and dove, and emerged just a few feet from the bank. "It's pure like a virgin. Put your suit on and come on in."

"I said, get out. The water's dirty."

She backstroked away from me. "No!"

"If you don't get out, I'll drag you out."

She frowned and searched my face closely with her keen, sparkling eyes and decided to obey. She came close to shore, stood and extended her hand. I pulled her from the water, snatched her towel off a nearby bush and gave it to her.

"Here. Dry yourself and put your clothes on."

"What's wrong with you?"

"Nothing's wrong with me."

"You sound crazy."

SO LOVELY TO KILL

I laughed. "Yeah, crazy. The river is half blood. Your father and Dee just killed Causby. They—they dissected him up stream, if you like things brutal."

Whether she liked it or not, that was the way she got it.

"You're not very funny," she said at last, putting the towel to her face.

"I'm not trying to be."

In an instant she realized it. She dropped the towel, spun away from me, stumbled two or three yards and sank to her knees on the ground. She didn't cry. She didn't utter a sound. She just knelt there. Her hands clutched at the grass and her eyes stared vacantly into the night. So I had been brutal. How else can you say such a thing? It's worse when you lead up to it.

"Just now?" she asked.

"A while back. An hour or so ago."

She looked at me then, her coldness her most salient feature. As quickly as that she was gone from me, vanished behind the protective shell that allowed her escape from the world. It was her way, almost instinctive, of confronting those forces that were too great and too powerful for her to cope with. Yet, she was still fighting.

"What happens now?" she asked.

I didn't trust her enough to become Johnny Fury to her, but gave her a chance. She could take it or leave it.

"I'm getting out," I said. "I came to take you with me, if you want to come."

Her look was malicious, sub-zero in ferocity. "And then you go to the cops, huh?"

I didn't reply. Her remark made no utterance appropriate. I moved forward, stopped and stared down at her. I watched the pale moonlight slice through the trees and play softly over her bikini, white against her tan skin.

SO LOVELY TO KILL

Strangely, the fact that she had penetrated my masquerade had trouble gaining a foothold in my mind. It was a thing we had in common—I had never believed in Apple Renney, either. And, of course, whatever he had been, Renney no longer existed. He was as dead as old Causby.

I reached down and my hands closed on her shoulders, gently. I said, "Think again, Carol—think hard. I'll go to the cops?"

Her mouth hardened. "You're not Renney," she said. "You'll go to the cops." Her lips quivered. "I won't—"

She never finished whatever she was trying to say. Suddenly she surrendered. Her shoulders sagged and her head rolled limply. She cried softly, like a child afraid of the dark. I knelt beside her and took her hand.

"How did you know?" I asked. "How did you guess I wasn't Renney?"

She waited a long time. Finally she whispered, "It's very simple, really—the real Renney is—was—crazy."

I said, "Tell me about it."

She was silent again for a long time. At last she said, "In—in Miami when Manie and the Marchettis were being tried. I heard Dee had gone down there. I had no one, so I followed. I was lucky. I found her."

"You found her?"

"With Renney. They were living together."

"Where?"

"In a motel."

"What happened?"

She pulled away from me and shed her bathing cap. Her hair streamed to her shoulders like molten starlight. She paused, breathed greedily and tried to compose herself. She was no longer hard. Shock had broken her.

"I went to the motel. To Dee's room. She told me to use it. This was in the afternoon. Dee had an errand in town. Renney came in. He was looking for her. He found me instead. We talked a little, and he didn't seem to me as bad as he had been painted. I listened to him, trying to understand the stories I'd heard. Then he made a couple of passes—well, any girl gets used to that. I thought I'd put him down when—"

She stopped. Her eyes went wide in recollection. There was terror in her look—and something else. Suddenly she whispered, "I can't—I can't—"

I slid my arm around her. There was a shared terror in me. I made myself say, "It's over and done with, whatever it was. It's dead and buried, gone."

She collapsed against me. Not because I meant anything to her. Not because of anything I said. Just because she needed to collapse.

Suddenly her voice was almost normal. "I guess—it was nothing, really. It's happened to all sorts of girls, not just Manie's daughter. Anyway, suddenly Renney was a wild man. Insane. He must have been a maniac—around women, I mean. He locked the door." She paused to look at me. "Oh, you talk like him and look like him—but he's crazy, obsessed. In that room he was—what do you want me to say?"

"Whatever you feel you have to say."

"He raped me," she said.

It choked me. It killed me. But what I said was, "Okay, you've told me. What happened next?"

"I ran away, that's all." She shrugged angrily. "I went as far as I could. I didn't go far enough. When Manie was acquitted he sent the Marchettis after me. I've run away twice since." She reflected half philosophically, half with revulsion: "When Manie wants to find you, he's more efficient than the police."

I left her and strode to the water's edge. I stopped being

123

a tough guy. I had the information I wanted. As I unscrambled her story I stared across the pool at the deep shades of black and silver—and realized I hadn't erred, coming to the river. It was all right. She was on my side.

Now the question was—was I on hers?

Carol rose, retrieved her towel and then slumped to the earth once more. She began to dry herself, but her toilet was interrupted by a fresh flood of tears. The evening had been too much even for her rigid controls—even she could not escape murder.

I kept silent. If she thought I was police, it was just as well. I still had to protect myself. Manie had too many homicidal friends and until he was in jail or strapped in the chair I didn't want my real identity bouncing around the countryside. No hero I.

I laid my hand on her damp cheek and whispered, "It's okay, kid. It's okay. Let's try to forget it now. Get into your clothes. We have a long walk ahead of us."

Her arms suddenly hooked around my neck and she pulled my cheek to hers. "Oh, God," she said. "I just can't tell you everything—I just can't—"

"It's all right," I said. "You've said enough."

We sat in silence. After a while I kissed her. There was no passion in the kiss, no lust, not the slightest hint or desire. Neither of us spoke, and a warmth built between us—a great and growing need of closeness.

I was not sure at that moment that it wasn't love, that what followed was not the final commitment I had avoided with Agnes. I know that we finally slipped away from the world as we knew it tonight, that our awareness merged in each other . . . we kissed again, and it was like nothing I had known before. Nor was what followed like anything I had known before . . . I am not sure that the earth moved, but when it was still again, the two of us had responded to a new creation. Not until then did we feel the world again, the damp moss coverlet on the ground chilling the length of our bodies, and the faint breeze that trickled through the trees.

We said nothing afterwards, for a long time, but simply clung together. Finally I whispered, "We've got to go away, Carol—that's why I came, remember?"

She nodded. "Yes." She did not move immediately. After a while she shivered—reality had crowded back upon her. "I have to go back for my clothes. I didn't bring anything but my bathing suit."

We walked hand in hand, absorbed once more in the horror waiting for us back at the farm, but with a new bond of discovery between us. Once she said, "Can it really happen like this between two people? I—I don't even know who you really are."

I said, "It can—and you'll know in time."

She gave me a strange look, and for an instant I thought she was going to retreat behind her own private iron curtain again. Then her fingers pressed mine, and the moment had passed.

"I know I will," she whispered. "And right now it doesn't seem to matter—"

We reached the barn and slipped silently into the blackness of the ground floor. Holding my hand tightly, she led me up the stairs. We reached the door, but she didn't open it right then.

Instead she leaned against me and whispered, "Kiss me!"

I did.

She broke away abruptly, pushed the door open and went in. I followed her, and was totally unprepared for her quick lunge to one side. She grabbed the door and slammed it shut behind me.

SO LOVELY TO KILL

I said in surprise, "What's the—"

I didn't finish. I glanced toward the window. Sitting in a rocking chair beside it, his features sharply outlined by a splash of moonlight, was a friend of mine. It was Patty Sears, and his big gun was pointing at me.

16

I DIDN'T have to be asked. Voluntarily, I thrust my hands in the air. The gun looked as big as an artillery piece and twice as lethal. It didn't waver. It was steady, beaded on my vulnerable middle. Patty sucked on a cigarette and the pink glow illuminated his pudgy features. He said nothing. I watched Carol move away from me and fall on the bed. Patty laughed.

Oh, it was funny, all right. Real boff! Only I couldn't share it.

I peered at Carol and no hate was more deadly than mine. I had loved her for a moment, had thought we both had found something we had not found elsewhere. Now it was gone and gone, too, were a few layers of my pride.

Patty continued to laugh. To him I must have looked funy as hell.

He broke off finally, to ask Carol "Has he got anything on him?"

She rolled over on her stomach. "No gun, if that's what you mean."

Patty stepped forward and grinned. "Where's Renney?"

"Who?"

He waved the gun. "I don't want questions, Fury. Renney? What happened to him?"

So he knew my name. I said, "Go to hell."

"Sure, if that's the way you want it." He shrugged his narrow shoulders. "But after you."

Carol propped her chin in her hands and dug her elbows into the mattress. The bathing suit sagged and it didn't do a thing to me. She said, "I'm sorry, Johnny. Really sorry."

"You can—" I didn't say it. No word could have said what I wanted to say. I put my attention on Patty.

I was staring at blue steel, at a young cannon with six slugs in its belly, aimed at mine. This was very important, I told myself, more important than Carol's defection, and I wondered why there were only three of us in the room, why Manie and Dee and the Marchettis weren't there?

I said, "I thought I got by you, Patty."

"In jail?" He nodded. "You did. You fooled me good. You just didn't get by Carol. She's a smart kitten."

"She's not too bright if she rang you in on it," I said.

He took offense and spat, "You son of a bitch!" and gave me a slash across the cheek with the barrel of the gun. He stepped back quickly. I felt the pain scorch through my head.

Carol squirmed and giggled. "I *am* a stinker, Johnny. I never met Apple in Miami. I never met him in all my life."

I kept my mind off her—and on his gun. And on the puzzle of how they had known.

Then my eye fell on the telephone, an extension from the main house, a vicious black monster that sat there as a symbol of my carelessness. I knew now what had happened. When I had called Matt, Carol had lapped up the entire conversation. The rest had been simple. She had had plenty of time to prepare for our rendezvous at the river.

SO LOVELY TO KILL

I burned again when I thought of it. I said to Patty, "This is a little out of your line, isn't it?" I didn't think you went in for guns."

"I'd do a helluva lot for a half million dollars."

So this was another little team after Manie's bazooka money. "You and Carol?" I said. "Manie isn't going to like it."

"Manie ain't ever going to know."

"Sure," I said. "It will be easy to keep a thing like that a secret."

A reply was postponed. The room, suddenly, was buried in darkness. I could have sworn that someone had climbed up and turned off the moon.

"Stay where you are," Patty said. "I can see you."

I didn't think he could, but I wasn't going to chance it. He was less than five feet away and I had the uncomfortable feeling that the gun hadn't moved. I heard Carol brush away from the bed and, as she did, the room was flooded with moonlight again.

She was at the window. "It's going to rain," she said. "Clouds. Big, black ones."

Already, I could hear the whir of the wind.

"Put a light on," said Patty.

She did, after pulling down the shades. She returned to the bed and sat on its edge. "A storm will make it perfect," she said. "We'll wait until it really pours and then you can go back to the house, Johnny. No one will hear you."

I laughed. "Why kid me, Carol. Instead, tell me how you are going to do it. Do I get it between the eyes?"

She stood, grinned, paced in a wide circle and came around behind me. Gingerly, caressingly, she placed her hands on my cheeks.

She said, "Johnny, darling, you're not going to die.

SO LOVELY TO KILL

You're going to live, and probably for a long, long time.
You're in this, too, you know, and we need you badly."

I was looking into Patty's eyes. "The minute I'm out
of this barn I'll run like hell."

"I don't think you will," said Carol. "Patty, show him."

He backed away from me, grinning, and kicked open
the bathroom door, snapped on the light.

In that shocking, crushing instant, I felt like a brother
to death. All vitality drained from me and I scarcely
felt Carol's ghoulishly caressing hands on my face, barely
heard her mocking laughter.

As though in a trance I watched Patty turn his gun
from me and level it on a trussed figure on the bathroom
floor.

It was Agnes. Wide strips of adhesive tape bound her
arms behind her. Her ankles were taped, and another
strip sealed her mouth. Her black hair was disarranged,
but what dominated everything were her two huge,
frightened eyes.

How had she gotten here?

"All right?" Patty rasped. "Do we get along, Fury?"

It took every ounce of willpower for me not to tear
into him. Mine was a dangerous anger that swayed me
like a tide—in that instant, I was ready to kill. I started
toward him, stopped and started again. Once I saw Patty's
finger whiten on the trigger.

I stood still finally, helplessly. "Okay," I said. "You've
got me."

Still, it seemed incredible that they should have brought
her here simply to put pressure on me. One thing stood
out—they had kidnapped. That meant they were playing
for keeps. I said nothing to Agnes, gave her no reassurance
beyond what she could read in my eyes. Words would have
been pointless.

130

SO LOVELY TO KILL

I turned to Patty. "What do you want me to do?"

He waited a while before answering. Outside the world became alive. Large drops of rain began to splatter the roof and a crack of thunder shook the countryside. In a few minutes we would be in the center of a tempest.

"Go back to the house," Patty said. "In the morning, get 'em out of the house—the whole tribe. I don't give a damn how you do it, but get 'em to town and keep them there."

"I don't get it," I said.

"You don't have to," he told me with a grin.

But of course I got it. They had figured out, as I had, where the bazooka loot was hidden—they wanted a clear field of operations while getting it out.

"What about her?" I asked, nodding over my shoulder at Agnes.

"We'll let her go," Carol said.

"Sure," said Patty. "It's a promise."

It was a promise, I thought, they wouldn't keep. They hadn't brought her here for my sake alone, I was sure. But all I could do now was stall for time.

"I want to talk to her," I said, and Patty stood aside.

I pushed down a wave of guilt and took Agnes into my arms. She was cold, frightened, despite the warm night. Her black eyes suffered at me.

"They're not interested in us, baby," I told her. "Not really. Just the money."

She nodded, not confidently, and I held her tightly for a moment. This must have bothered Carol. She moved to the door and her lips were contorted.

She said, "That's all very touching, Johnny. But now you'd better get moving."

I stood up. I stalked past her and through the door.

131

17

I slipped out of the barn into the wet ebony night. The sky had opened up and a black torrent of water smothered the earth. It was accompanied by wicked claps of thunder close by and from far off came rumbling replies. Spasmodically, the lightning illuminated the fields and knolls as brightly as high noon.

I ran.

I got soaked.

I slipped into the farmhouse and climbed the stairs. I didn't have to worry about noise; the old house rattled rheumatically as the wind smacked against it—the racket would have covered a troop of cavalry. Somewhere a shutter banged and some recess in the construction produced a whistle, a moan, ghostly and eerie like the mating call of spirits.

The hallway was black. I couldn't see, but I was aware of the turbulent movement of the dank atmosphere. It stirred heavily, each gust of moisture-laden wind feeling on my cheeks and arms like the brushing of bats' wings. I felt a slave to the discomfort. I no longer had a will. Once there had been a chance for me to run. Now, a threat to the girl I almost had loved kept me here.

Much of what I felt stemmed from a sense of guilt. I had all but forgotten Agnes since coming here—yet I had

SO LOVELY TO KILL

taken her to a public place during out last evening together, and someone must have seen us. Once Carol had
warned Patty Sears of my identity, it wouldn't have been
difficult to connect me to Agnes. Her peril was on my
conscience.

I reached my door and groped for the match I had
wedged there. I found it on the floor—so my absence had
been detected, and some pretty glib explanations would
be needed. Manie and Dee now knew that I hadn't been
in my room all night—perhaps they guessed that I had
seen them kill Causby.

I opened the door, and some of my worry vanished.
I knew that Manie hadn't missed me. Dee had. She was
in my room. She sat in my only chair, her hands behind
her head. She wore a robe over her nightgown, and remembering her on the night of my arrival I was willing
to concede that this was almost a formal visit. There
was an oddly angelic look about her, and remembering
how she had looked killing Causby, I felt ill.

I eased the door shut, feeling the sickness bubble high
in my throat, and said, "What are you doing here?"

She ignored my question. "Where have you been?"

"I couldn't sleep, so I took a walk."

"What kind of a walk?"

"How many kinds are there? I couldn't sleep, so I
took a walk."

"Where?"

"Along the road out front."

"Oh." She seemed satisfied.

"How long have you been here?" I asked.

"An hour," she whispered. "By God, it seemed like
a year."

"Well, I'm here," I said.

"Yes, you're soaking wet."

133

"I know. I got caught. Storms come up quickly around here."

I sat on the edge of the bed. "Don't you think you're taking a chance?" I asked. "This isn't exactly brilliant, you know."

"It's as bright as I can be tonight," she said. "God, what a hell of night! But Manie couldn't sleep and took sleeping pills. We're safe. He'll be out for hours." Something seemed to catch in her throat. "I had to see you, Apple—Manie plans a doublecross."

I laughed. I couldn't help it. God knows what he'd expected, but what Causby got would pass as a doublecross anywhere. She wasn't telling me news.

"How?" I asked. It seemed a good question. I doubted she'd give me a good answer.

"You're dripping all over. Get your clothes off."

"The hell with that. You're dressed—I'm dressed. We're going to stay that way." I remember thinking that right then, rather than knuckling down to her, I would have to let her stick her knife into me, if she had one. She was like those crawling things you find under logs.

She seemed to read my thoughts. "You're an idiot," she said. "You shouldn't have mentioned being able to fence off that money—it's something Manie hasn't been able to do. Now he thinks you're bigger than he is. He's afraid of you. He plans to ditch you."

"How?"

"He's pulling the bank job tomorrow. First thing in the morning, before you're up. He wants to do it without you."

It didn't take me long to get it. I laughed again, without a real reason. Manie could be blundering into trouble—Matt Nugent had alerted the local cops. On the other hand, I had to stick with him, and now I would be on my own. There was no chance to warn Matt.

134

Dee asked, "What's so funny?" and that brought me back.

I said, "Go back and tell Manie nobody doublecrosses Apple Renney. He can't cut me out now!"

She said, "Are you crazy? I told you he took sleeping pills. I couldn't wake him if—"

"Then I'll be there in the morning."

Surprisingly, she giggled. "Manie'll be awfully mad." She came over to me, laid her head on my chest and her hands held me. "Apple—" she said.

She was warm against me and I could feel her body throbbing, her heart pounding against my ribs.

I said, "Huh?"

"You've changed—I'm not sure I don't like you even better this way. You're not rough, like you used to be."

"I've been sick," I told her. "But I'm coming back— and I'm still rough enough to take care of Manie for you."

She sighed. "Apple, honey—"

"Yes?"

"I've been thinking about the Marchettis. For a long time."

"What about them?"

"I don't think we'll have to kill them." It was a concession. "I think they'll fold once Manie is dead," she went on. "They'd be sort of lost without him. You know what I mean?"

"No."

"I mean that once we kill Manie we'll just tell them he skipped with the bazooka money or just plain skipped, and that's all there'll be to it. They'll lose heart if they can't trust Manie."

I got the drift then. We were back on the "kill Manie" kick. She must have wanted Manie's death badly, if she was ready to forget the Marchettis.

135

I didn't expect the rest. Dee pushed closer to me, crushing me in her arms with her unwomanly strength.

"Apple?"

"Huh?"

"We killed Causby tonight—Manie and I."

This rocked me down to my heels. God—she was really insane! I had thought her mad when she plunged the knife into Causby's chest, but this—to want to talk about it . . .

"We had to, you know. He was getting nosy about the money."

Sure, I thought. The money. He cut down a dead, rotting apple tree I had mentioned to him by accident. I remembered the look he gave me as he went back to finish the job, and suddenly, for no other reason, I thought him an honest man.

I said, "What do you mean, I know? You never told me where the money was. You never trusted me. How the hell would I know why you had to kill Causby? Look, I'm soaked. I've been sick. I've got to get to bed."

But there was more. She insisted now on talking about it, indulging in a fantastic description of strangulation and burial, the direct opposite of what had really happened, except that they certainly had killed him. Not once during her discourse was she truly concentrating on her words. She was reliving the actual scene, responding to the thrill all over again, but reassuring herself that she had done the right thing, because Causby was dangerous and had to die and they had killed him.

Afterwards she wanted to make love.

"Look, Dee," I said adamantly. "I'm tired and I've been sick."

"You're really changing, Apple. You're not the same."

"I told you, I've been sick."

136

SO LOVELY TO KILL

"Never that sick."

"Sick," I said and I didn't move. I didn't breathe. And I really was sick. There was an acid taste in my mouth and I was cold.

She got it finally.

She left.

18

THE LUMINOUS dots on my wrist watch told me it way four-thirty-seven when Dee left the room. Outside, the world was exploding. Water fell from the laden skies in a solid mass and the wind lashed it against the side of the house.

I was tired and sleep might have overtaken me despite everything. I didn't give it a chance. I smoked butt after butt, sitting in the chair next to the window. Slowly, sluggishly, dawn stretched its wan fingers across the land. With the light I saw the water as silver knives, spearing downward. Overhead was a low ceiling of black clouds that promised to remain there all day.

During a brief lull I caught the faint tinkle of Manie's alarm clock. I dressed, completely this time, with a heavy automatic straining at the bottom of my pocket. Maybe it gave me a false sense of security, but without it I would have been panic-stricken. I left my room and thumped down the stairs.

No one was there. I waited, standing in the middle of the living room. I didn't think about the worst of what could happen. I just tried not to think.

The four of them descended on tiptoe and when they reached the landing, they bumped together like stooges in a pie-throwing comedy. All except Dee were pop-eyed. I almost laughed.

Manie finally rolled forward, stopped and glared at me. "What are you doing up so early?" It was an honest, unadorned question. Confused, he really wanted to know.

"It's a nice rainy day," I said. "A good day to pull a bank job. Rain can cover a lot of tracks, you know."

He thought a minute. "Yeah, that's not a bad idea."

"Of course, you didn't have this in mind," I said venomously.

"I was thinking about it," he said, and stormed into the kitchen.

Dee plunked on the sofa undaintily and exposed half of the white flesh of her thigh. The Marchettis looked at one another and Tee-hee laughed.

I followed Manie into the kitchen. There was an open whiskey bottle on the table, apparently left over from last night. This morning, Manie wasn't having any. Alternately he guzzled milk from a bottle and stared out at the mean day. I could almost read his thoughts. He was thinking that he was stuck with me, but didn't know just what to do about it.

I said, "The troopers still got you worried, Manie?"

He glared at me. "Yeah, they got me worried." He added wisely: "If they're at the bank, we'll forget it. Then maybe you can go back to the coast where you belong."

"I still got a good deal for you, Manie."

He didn't answer, but he was thinking about it.

I pushed him further. "It will simplify things, Manie, if you fence off that dough. We could even forget about the bank job."

"We're pulling the bank job and we'll do it the way you planned."

I leaned against the door jamb and said, "Where's the old guy?"

139

"He went to visit his sister," he answered quickly.

"When?"

"Last night, late."

"Damn funny time."

"Shut up, will you!"

"Sure, Manie, if that's the way you want it."

I strode to a clothes tree in the corner of the kitchen and stripped it of an old raincoat which had belonged to Causby, draped it over my shoulders, then grabbed the set of stolen Jersey license plates from the top of the cupboard. I started for the back door.

Manie blocked my way. "Where do you think you're going?" he asked.

"To the barn. I'll put them on the car."

"That's my job."

"It was," I said coldly, and slipped past him and into the deluge. Fortunately, he didn't follow. But I wondered if an itchy finger was wrapped around the trigger of his gun as he stared at me through the window.

Manie had rigged the plates with elastic tape, so it was a simple matter to slip them on. I worked quickly, then dashed upstairs and hammered on Carol's door. There was no response, so I banged a few more times. Another wait and finally the door cracked open. Carol, red-eyed and sleepy, peeked out at me. Her hand was behind her back and I had a hunch she held a gun, too.

I didn't waste time with a lengthy explanation. "We're pulling the bank job today."

Slowly she absorbed it and nodded and I bounced down the stairs and out of the barn. Within an hour, I knew, she and Patty would be hacking at the cement in the trees.

When I got back into the house I detected a noticeable change. Maybe the four of them had slipped in a quick

140

conference. Manie came up to me, shuffled meekly and smiled, "Well, Apple, I guess we're all set."

"I am," I said. I waved toward the outside. "Let's go. I wouldn't want to miss this for anything."

We got off immediately, unceremoniously. We carried little equipment—Manie and the Marchettis had face masks, made from an old sheet. We all had guns. We carried no umbrellas, had no raincoats, or rubbers—nothing that would have been appropriate on such a day.

Dee drove and Manie sat next to her. I was in the back with the Gila monsters and at first no one said a word. Then, a little past the driveway Manie snapped, "Stop the car!"

I slipped my hand into my pocket and wrapped my fingers around the handle of my automatic. I was so tense that I released the safety.

I shouldn't have worried. He wasn't interested in me but rather in a wet, weed-filled field that paralleled the road. I peered out the window, wiping the condensation away with my hand, and saw what had attracted his attention. Toward the forest, partially hidden by weeds and shrubs, was a blue Ford coupe. I was sure it belonged to Patty Sears. Apparently he arrived at night and hadn't been able to hide it too well. The question was, would Manie recognize it?

"What the hell is that doing there?" he said.

"What?" said Dee.

"That damned car, back in the woods there."

They all saw it and stared and no one seemed interested.

"Probably some nut," said Seymour, "fishing downstream."

"In this weather?"

"Guys that fish are nuts."

141

Manie's face tightened. "I don't like the idea of somebody snooping around."

"The hell with it," said Dee. "He can't hurt us."

Manie swore, half to himself, but apparently he was convinced. He grunted and we got rolling again. I felt the tension pass out of my body and could almost relax. Strangely, the bank job had become a minor operation.

My allegiance had shifted to Carol and Patty. I was rooting that they'd succeed. They had to. I figured that it would take us at least an hour to get to the Winslow, an hour to pull the job, an hour to get back. That totaled three hours. It should be enough. If it was, maybe I'd see Agnes again.

Visibility was poor and I thought that Dee was pushing the car too fast. The world was a gray blur as the slow minutes crept by. There was a steady liquid swishing as the Buick wheeled forward like a war machine.

Presently there was conversation and it was serious. They realized, whether they liked it or not, that I was with them, that a bank was to be robbed and that I was going in cold. This wouldn't do. I had to be informed.

Most of it I knew already from yesterday's rehearsals. The bank had been built around 1930. I was familiar with the architecture and knew that the alarm system would be hidden in the walls. I already had some ideas on how to knock it out—if I succeeded, our only worry would be the bank employees and those few customers caught inside, all rigid under the persuasion of drawn guns.

If I failed, the job would be called off. As Manie said, "We'll just take off without you." They would, too.

But failure was not on their minds. As we hit the main approach to Winslow they had dollar signs for eyes. After I did my work, I was to return to the street and take care of the traffic cop. Manie and the Marchettis would take over inside the bank.

Dee would be parked halfway up the block. Manie would signal me, I would pass it on to Dee and she would meet us at the front door with the car. We would be off.

Theoretically.

"Do it right, boy," Manie said, warming up, "and we'll be pals for life."

I let him have it his way. It might be a short life.

We arrived in Winslow at eigth-thirty, a half hour before the bank was scheduled to open. The rain was heavier and the wind was picking up. Dee drove around the block and we studied the setting. The bank was a little newer than their description had indicated and I was impressed by the sturdy picture it presented. The building was long and squat, the facade a rich Craigmar marble that sparkled as the water ran down its sides. The state troopers weren't there and Manie grunted his approval.

The lone traffic cop had dismissed his duties and was standing under the protective marquee. He looked cold, huddled in his black rubber raincoat. With irritation, he swung his billy back and forth—he was interested mainly in the weather. The streets looked deserted. A few shop-keepers stood in their doorways and gazed dolefully at a day that would bring them few sales.

Dee pulled to the curb two blocks from the bank. She let the motor idle. In front of us the windshield wiper swished back and forth. A kid in a yellow raincoat dashed down the street. He didn't look at us and seemed happy to be out in the wind and the rain. We said nothing. We waited.

At five after nine the red patrol car arrived, parked in front of the bank and a group of men piled out. They were vague, contorted, moving figures in the rain. They entered the bank and exited. They did this three times, climbed back into the patrol car and immediately it pulled away. It swept around the corner and out of sight.

Manie said hoarsely, "That's the dough. Get moving, Apple."

I said, "Give me ten minutes and don't walk. People run when it rains."

Manie piled out, crossed the street and stood under the awning in front of a haberdashery shop. Seymour and Tee-hee scurried to a real estate building and bunched themselves in the doorway.

Dee dropped me off at the bank, then continued around the block.

I entered the bank. The place wasn't big. but I felt as though I were standing in the middle of Yankee Stadium. The main floor, bleak with blue light, was virtually empty. A middle-aged woman was standing in front of a writing table, filling out a slip. She was fat and uncomfortably drenched. Two tellers were in their cages, preparing for the day's business. The girl behind the savings window just sat there. She looked at me.

With one sweeping glance, I took in everything—the tall, rain-streaked windows to the left and the cages to the right. Beyond were three offices belonging to the president, vice-president and the treasurer.

The vault was set in the back wall and the mammoth steel door was open. Inside, two clerks were opening the money sacks which held the race track take. To the left of the vault was a stairway to the basement. A sign read: SAFETY DEPOSITS, and an arrow pointed the way.

I strode to the staircase. I felt as though a thousand eyes were on me and I expected to be challenged. I wasn't.

The staircase gave off a sandpaper sound as I de-

144

scended into the basement. I entered a small alcove. To the rear was the safety deposit section. It consisted of several narrow corridors branching away from the main aisle. The entire section was fronted by heavy iron bars. On the inside, to the left of the door, was a desk. No one was there. A hand-lettered sign said, "Ring for Attendant."

I rang.

What I would do next wasn't clear in my mind. Somehow I had to get inside, find the fuse box. I knew the attendant would ask me for an identification card and I knew I didn't have one. What I did have was a gun. I slipped my hand in my pocket and stroked the cold metal. It didn't give me much comfort.

From deep inside the vaults I heard a pair of feet scrape down another flight of stairs. I waited stoically and I wondered at my composure.

The attendant broke into view and I felt relieved. She was a girl, barely past twenty. She was not pretty, but looked wholesome. Her black hair was crisp and curled close to her head, defying the dank day. She greeted me pleasantly.

"How do you do, sir. May I see your I.D. card?"

I smiled, pulled out Apple Renney's wallet and began to fumble with the many cards he had stuffed inside the leather compartments.

Slowly I said, "I'm a new depositor and I don't have these things straight yet."

She gave me an understanding smile and waited. I chose a card and purposely dropped it. It fluttered inside the bars. I couldn't reach it. She gave me a look, took out a key, started to unlock the gate.

When she turned around, I had my gun out.

"No noise!" I said. "Nothing! Do you understand?"

She stiffened, so petrified she couldn't move.

145

SO LOVELY TO KILL

"Let's go," I said. "Where's the fuse box? Come on, girlie. Get with it!"

Trembling, she led the way.

We hurried down the main corridor, then swung to the right at the end. The fuse box was back against the wall. I made a quick inspection and moaned. In addition to the regular lock, a padlock as big as a fist dangled from the box cover.

"Do you have the keys?" I asked.

She held her head in her hands and cringed in the corner. She didn't answer me until I went over and slapped her. Not hard.

"Damn it, do you have the keys?"

Her lower lip quivered and she shook her head. "H—honest, mister. Only the janitor has one."

The box was heavy and it wouldn't be easy to force it. The only thing I could do was attempt to bend a corner back. I went to work with the gun and my hands, using the gun barrel for purchase against the sharp edge of the box cover.

I broke my hands on it, but finally one corner of the box gave. I got my bleeding fingers into the aperture and pulled. Saliva flowed into my mouth and I was drenched with perspiration. The lid gave, slowly. Then the metal cawed loudly, yielding protestingly. I exhaled and wondered if the noise had been heard above the chatter of the storm outside.

The fuses were partially exposed. But which one controlled the alarm system? I forced my hand into the box and groped around for the code sheet, customarily posted inside the cover. It was a good day for thieves. Miraculously, I got what I was after—just the upper corner of the code sheet, but the one that said: Alarm system—Fuse #1.

SO LOVELY TO KILL

I unscrewed the fuse, dropped it to the floor and ground it under my heel.

Then I jumped as though someone had started to probe my insides with a hot poker. There was the steady scrape of feet on bare stone. From the bowels of the basement it was impossible to judge their direction.

The girl dropped her hands and stared at me and we weren't thinking the same thing. For an instant her eyes brightened, until once again she saw my gun. She shuddered and I clapped my hand over her mouth. I was hoping she would faint. It would save me a lot of time and trouble.

I listened. The scraping stopped and the attendant's buzzer rang. My shoulders sagged and I exhaled a hurricane. It was a customer, not an employee. Still, there were two to take care of now and I could handle only one at a time. There was only one thing to do.

I whispered in the girl's ear, "No noise, honey. I'm going to tie you up. Take off your skirt."

Somehow she managed a nod and, testing, I pulled my hand an inch from her mouth. She was mute and I smiled, applauding her discretion. She unzipped her skirt and stepped out of it. I ripped it into strips and, working fast, bound and gagged her.

Then I left her.

As I approached the desk my hands began to ooze blood again. My customer was the fat babe whom I had seen upstairs. She eyed me critically, not bothering to hide her irritation, and I flashed her a toothpaste smile.

"I'm so sorry to have kept you waiting," I said. "I was delayed. A packing case fell on my hands."

This got her and compassion overflowed. "Oh, how nasty. I didn't mean—"

"It's perfectly all right," I said, holding out my hands.

"They look terrible, but it is nothing serious. May I see your I.D. card?"

She held it out to me, but I didn't take it. I did look at the name.

"Oh, yes, Mrs. Remson. Of course!" and I opened the barred door. "Won't you step in?"

She waddled forward like a muddy duck, fidgeting self-consciously, and I knew I couldn't pull the same trick on her as I had with the girl. The sight of a gun would have shocked her into the hereafter.

I said, "Won't you sit at the desk, Mrs. Remson? I won't be but a minute."

She felt sorry for me—up to a point. Apparently, she was in a hurry. "Well, it's just that—I mean—"

My grin was dazzling. "Tut-tut, Mrs. Remson. I have good news for you. Our bookkeeper made a mistake on your safe deposit box rental. You have a refund coming. So, if you'll just get comfortable for a moment, I'll—"

I let my words trail off and watched her irritation evaporate. Her next expression suggested that she was simply thrilled to know that the bank had made an error.

She gurgled in a juvenile way, "Well, of course, Mr.—"

"Renney," I said, as I locked her in the vaults. "Charles Apple Renney," and as soon as the words were out I forgot about her. I was climbing the stairs, wondering if the worst was over.

19

THE MARCHETTIS were already in the bank when I reached the main floor. Both were at different tables and were filling out what looked like withdrawal slips. Withdrawals. It seemed ironic.

I strolled casually, keeping both hands in my pockets. The fingers of my right hand were wrapped around the handle of my gun. The girl at the savings window was still doing nothing. Again, she looked at me.

As I approached the front door, Manie came in. He looked for a nod and I gave him one. Everything was okay. Immediately, his hand went under his hat for his mask and I knew that all three of them would be disguised before I reached the street.

The cop was still under the marquee and I moved up next to him, standing slightly to his rear. He still seemed to be worrying mostly about the weather.

"Lousy day, huh?" I said softly.

He half turned to look at me. "Stinks, mister. Really stinks."

He returned his attention to the street and I took another step forward, took out my automatic and buried it into the small of his back. Simultaneously, I squeezed his gun arm.

"Don't move, sonny, or you're dead!"

Like the faithful dog Tray, he didn't even breathe.

"Don't turn around and keep your hands down. You'll probably be thrilled to know that the bank is being robbed."

"Huh?"

I slipped my hand into the wide slit in his raincoat and disarmed him. I also relieved him of his billy and handcuffs.

"Put your hands behind your back," I instructed.

He decided to get brave. He spun around, trying to remember what they taught him in police school, and went for my gun and groin in one synchronized motion. He telegraphed his intentions and, had I really been a desperado, he would have been greeting his ancestors by their heavenly names. As it was, my knee protected my vitals and I exploded the billy on his temple. He staggered against the building.

This time he held still while I snapped his own bracelets on him.

Somewhere in the bank a woman screamed. No commotion followed, so I knew that Manie had things under control.

I bunched the young cop's raincoat in my fist and peered into his whiskerless face. "Now get this. Contact Matt Nugent of the New York police. Tell him Agnes is being held hostage on the farm. Do you hear?"

He stared stonily.

"Dammit, listen! I don't have time to explain. Matt Nugent of the New York police—"

I stopped. Into the thousand noises of the storm there came the overpowering screech of a siren. For a second I stood there, wondering what the devil was happening, then dashed into the street. A red patrol car was speeding down the main drag. The siren no longer wailed. The

150

doors were open and a sextet of lobsters were ready to dive out and do battle.

I didn't plan to hang around and the young cop had the same idea. He beat it away from the marquee, out of the line of fire.

Frantically, I motioned to Dee and she responded immediately. She got to me before the patrol car reached the bank, opened the door and I dove into the front seat.

"Take off!" I cried, and instinctively ducked. I expected a shower of bullets to make a sieve out of Manie's car, but somehow, we were ignored. Dee was flustered and her feet fumbled on the floorboard. Then hell began to break loose.

Tee-hee was the first out of the bank and his gun was barking. Thin streaks of flame scorched from the muzzle. His mask had fallen around his neck and he was carrying a pillow case bulging with greenbacks. I hardly heard the noise when his fire was returned—it was not something to hear. It was something to see, and remember. Tee-hee slumped to the pavement. He did not move. A few bills spilled out of the pillow case and stuck to the wet pavement.

Dee got the Buick rolling. It lurched crazily. I twisted around in the seat and saw Seymour dash out of the bank. He didn't have his gun and hadn't bothered with the money. Momentarily, he put the cops off guard, because his arms were held high in the air, but he wasn't standing still. Sprinting like blazes, he bolted through the line of police and ran after our fleeing car.

The guns chattered and Seymour pitched forward. He lay spread-eagled in the middle of the road. His hands were outstretched, as though pointing accusingly at Dee and me.

Dee raced around the corner and I could see nothing

151

more. I held my breath and listened. Staccato explosions sounded again and we knew what had happened. That would have been Manie!

"What the hell went wrong?" Dee screamed.

"Forget it. Just drive!"

"I don't think they know we were with them."

"A lobster back there knows. Drive!"

"Oh, God," she said. "God!"

She got around another corner somehow and pushed the pedal to the floor on the straightaway. I saw the speedometer inch up to fifty, sixty, sixty-five. She could drive well and we had a good head start. I jumped around in the seat and peered through the rear window. Nothing was following us. Not yet.

One thing I was glad I had done. I had given the young cop Matt's name—I hoped the message had penetrated. Matt Nugent would know what to do. He wasn't one for heroics and would play it cautiously.

"Maybe it's a break," said Dee, and her eyes were big and glassy. "They're all dead. There's just you and me now, Apple."

I didn't answer. Slowly, crudely, I was beginning to understand. It wasn't an accident that the police arrived when they had. True, Matt had alerted them, but the timing was too exact to have been handled long distance. That left just one answer.

Carol and Patty!

Their names swelled in my brain.

"Is this the getaway route we planned?" I snapped at Dee.

"Yes."

"Can we get off it somewhere, back to the road we took coming in?"

"Yes, at the next crossroad, but—"

152

SO LOVELY TO KILL

"No buts. Take it." I thought a minute. "No, don't take it. Go past it for a block and stop the car. We'll ditch the plates."

"Are you crazy? There's a main highway at the end of this road. We'll never get caught once we're on it. On it for two miles, then off—"

"Do as I say!"

She shrugged angrily, pushed it up to seventy, streaked past the crossroad and applied the brakes. The big car skidded to a halt. There were no houses around as I hopped out, pulled the phony plates off and left them on the road.

I took the wheel then, turned around and retreated to the crossroads.

"Which way do I turn?"

"Right."

I pressed my foot to the floorboard and the Buick picked up speed. The narrow road was bumpy and we bounced as if on a pogo stick. The windshield wipers couldn't clear the water off fast enough and added to this were the darkness and wildness of the day. The wind now whipped at hurricane velocity.

Dee said, her voice high pitched and unnatural, "Why couldn't we do it the way we planned?"

"There's somebody on this road I want to meet."

That would be either Carol or Patty. I strained ahead for a glimpse of Patty's blue Ford. The tip-off to the police was too perfect. Either Carol or Patty had been on the main drag when we entered the bank, and would be heading back to the farm now.

Dee said, "You're going to kill us. We can't go this fast on this road."

"We have to," I said. "Didn't it occur to you that there was a tip-off? That blue coupe in the weeds, remember?

It must have had something to do with it."

"Carol," she cried. "Is it Carol?"

She had made it easy for me. "I think so. Who the hell else is there?"

"Carol doesn't have the nerve. She couldn't do it."

"You just don't know Carol," I said. "For a half million bucks, she'd fly to the moon."

So would Dee and I knew I had hit on a convincing note. I glanced at her, and there was a sudden fierceness in her face.

"Faster!" she whispered. "Faster! Damn that little slut!"

A little later we hit the highway and approached Ogsinto. It was necessary to slow down. The wind was ripping shingles off the roofs of houses and scaling them through the air. Trees had fallen and twice we saw static blue flashes of electricity as exposed power cables danced from the tops of sturdy telephone poles.

About ten miles out of Ogsinto we caught up with what looked like Patty's car. I rode his bumper and yelled at Dee, "Can you see for sure who it is?"

Dee put her face to the windshield. "I can't see anything."

I tried to pass the blue car and it swung wide to the left. For a perilous minute we were bumping on the soft shoulder of the road. I got the car back on the macadam and swerved to the right and the Ford came over with me. Whoever was in the car handled it like an expert.

Dee, I noticed, had taken a pistol from her pocketbook. It looked like a lady's .25 caliber and what she planned to do with it was beyond me. In the meantime, she was my cheering section.

"Crash her! Crash her off the road."

"We'll crash, too."

SO LOVELY TO KILL

She didn't seem to care.

The blue car clung to the center for a short stretch and then, suddenly, pulled to the right. A fallen tree blocked the road partially. We made it, but a reaching branch cracked our windshield and whisked away the wiper. I drove with virtually no visibility.

My eyes ached with the effort to see through a web of cracked glass that was thick with water. I came up hard against the Ford's bumper. Both cars rattled from the impact and for several seconds we oscillated on the glossy pavement. I don't know how we held the road.

After that I let the blue coupe get away—my only hope now was to latch on to it on the curve that approached Causby's farm.

I kept an eye on landmarks and, with a mile to go, let the Buick out all it would take. My eyes clung to the vague smear of blue that glowed through the sweep of mist and rain. We hit the curve and I fought to stay on the right side. The blue coupe didn't bother. It stayed in the center of the road.

At the sharpest point of the curve, the coupe suddenly braked. I did, too, swerving to the outside to avoid the crash while the coupe straightened and took off on the straightaway. I hadn't anticipated the move and no longer had control of the car.

The Buick barreled off the road, through the wire fence and plunged into the fields. The shocker came when we crashed into a fortress of sturdy trees. I was bounced against the windshield and the roof of the car. I couldn't tell what was happening to Dee. Then I didn't know what happened to me, either. There was a big nothing.

20

I WAS HURT. I was bruised and bleeding and my head throbbed. I could hardly move and realized that the car was virtually wrapped around me. Steel splinters, like ugly sabers, imprisoned me.

Then I detected the heavy odor of gas and knew I had to move. I struggled out of my topcoat, which was hopelessly ensnared in the wreckage, braced my feet against the motor and writhed through the open door. My trousers, coat and most of my shirt stayed in the car, and I felt steel rip through the flesh of my leg. But I was outside and I was alive.

Dee had been thrown free and was lying unconscious on her back. Her purse was still on her arm. But there wasn't a bruise on her that I could see.

I don't know why I bothered to do it, but I grabbed Dee and dragged her back and away from the car. In the next instant, the gasoline caught fire and the tank exploded. I fell flat to the ground as the car huffed into a mushroom of heat and flame. I grabbed Dee again, pushed back another ten or fifteen yards, and just lay there, panting and hurting. I watched Dee's eyes flicker. I watched her become thankful that she was still alive.

She kneaded her arms and legs, rolled over on her hands and knees, fighting shock.

SO LOVELY TO KILL

It might be too late for that, I thought dully. I struggled upright and left Dee kneeling there.

I fought my way up the black macadam road, occasionally losing my footing and sprawling on all fours. Once I ducked a branch that came whistling through the air, and my own weight carried me to the ground. I staggered erect and fought forward again.

I paused only once to look back at Dee. She hadn't moved. She was still trying to shake the dizziness out of her brain.

I reached the driveway and the mud sucked off my shoes and socks. Patty's blue car was parked at the side of the barn. One open door flapped like a wing and the barn was taking a beating, too. Windows were broken and the front door had been blown away. The main house had fared no better. It's shingles were almost gone, the front porch had given way, sagging low, a casualty of storm and age.

I ran low, zigzagging like a foot soldier leaving a hedgerow, half expecting a bullet, and dove to what was left of the porch. On my hands and knees I crawled inside, silently cursing myself for not having taken Dee's gun.

The hallway was empty and so were the living room and kitchen on the first floor. I gulped air into my lungs and tried to shake off the fatigue and fear.

My hands were raw and crimson. My right arm was bleeding and so was my leg. I limped back into the kitchen and jammed the telephone receiver tight to my ear, attempting to cut off the clamoring day. As I might have expected, the instrument was dead. The lines were down.

Then I saw Patty. I could see him through the kitchen window. He was in the orchard, hacking away at the

157

trees. His motions were frantic—when you're trying to beat somebody out of a hot half-million, they've a right to be.

I didn't wait. Just for show, I grabbed Causby's old, unloaded shotgun from behind the front door, and inched out again into the storm. I ran, using one tree after another for cover against both the second story windows of the barn and against Patty who, as he swung at the cement with a small sledge, had his back to me. He was working feverishly, angrily—maybe, I thought, with a touch of despair. I could guess why. Most of the trees I passed had been gouged of cement, which meant that Patty had been laboring steadily, if without success.

The thought struck me—he had failed as we all had failed. The money was not in the trees, or he would have recovered some of it by this time. I watched him heft the sledge and I knew that long ago he must have realized this. It was just one of those things. He *knew*, but there were still other trees. He had to go on.

I was sure of how I felt. Not disappointed, exactly. The damned money was not worth the aggravation, not worth the danger to Agnes and me. Certainly not worth death.

I edged closer and Patty saw me. He spun around, panting, looking like a cornered feline. He was wet, bruised and dirty and his hands seemed to be swollen to twice their normal size.

I leveled the shotgun shoulder high and took another step forward. Patty Sears made no counter-offensive. He retreated instead, slowly at first—finally he turned and ran. I loped after him and, because of my driving anger, I think, caught him. I don't think Patty went more than twenty strides before I caught him with a flying tackle, cleanly.

SO LOVELY TO KILL

He had something driving him, too—panic, perhaps. At any rate, he surprised me. Before I had my wind back, he was out of my grasp and on his feet; and that small sledge arched at my head. It caught me on the shoulder, numbingly, and gave him all the time he needed. He swung again and this time landed glancingly on the side of my head.

I did not lose consciousness, because the blow wasn't solid. But it was good enough to end the battle and I sank into a hazy, torturous void. I was aware of my hurt, my helplessness and unable to do anything about either. If he had had the courage of a killer then, he could have finished me.

I waited for the final blow—it never came. Instead, presently, my eyes focused and I began to feel the wind and the rain again. The wetness stung my face and flooded my eyes and there was the vague shape of a tree and a dark bundle of clouds and, immediately, an explosion in my brain. The pain had broken through—and along with the agony came voices.

"Johnny! Johnny!"

It was Agnes, and for a moment she said no more, just held me tightly, her cheek on my cheek, rocking me back and forth in her arms.

"Johnny, Johnny," she said. "What were you trying to do?"

"I wasn't doing too well," I admitted weakly and now I clung to her, fighting off a wave of nausea. I groaned aloud.

"I got away, Johnny, do you hear me? I got away."

"I hear," I said. I tried to smile. "You're quite a gal, but where's Carol? What happened to her?"

"She's where I was, tied up. It was a hot night, Johnny, and damp. It sort of softened the adhesive and I

159

worked all night until my wrists were free. But I was afraid to do anything until now, until I saw you and Patty."

I swore—Patty! I had forgotten about him. "Where did he go, did you see?"

She pointed toward the river. "He just ran, Johnny."

"Let's go see why," I said. I was wondering why the river. What was down there? I stood up.

She said, "Do you think you're able?"

"I'm able."

"But you can't, Johnny. He has a gun."

I didn't think so. "He would have used it if he had one."

She seemed uncertain but finally fell in step beside me.

We moved along, but we didn't run. My body was no longer geared for speed. My head was still a chamber of agony and my limbs were weak and rubbery.

We reached the river and that was what it had finally become—it was no longer a lazy, churning stream. It was a miniature Niagara, proud of its great swells that rumbled downward and off to the flanks where they overflowed the banks and the footpath. The water boiled a deep, angry brown.

We came upon the tombstones, went around them and reached what was once Carol's secret playground. The pool had spread to twice its normal size. There was no sign of Patty, and I knew he could not have gone beyond the pool.

The only logical explanation was that he had given us the slip along the way, probably hiding behind thick foliage until we had passed. He had doubled back on us— the trick of a hunted animal—and I had been too dull to foresee it.

I was too spent to do anything about it now. We took refuge under a generous spread of leafy bushes. They

160

offered some protection.

At that moment Agnes had the greater strength. I felt as though I had been running, working, fighting for forty-eight hours and, when I thought about it, that was exactly what I had been doing. But I was merely spent—not licked.

Despite her disheveled appearance, Agnes looked good to me. Her hands probing my hurts with a professional thoroughness, were comforting.

"Tell me what happened, Johnny."

I told her everything as quickly as I could, but I didn't bother with the whys and wherefores—just the facts. She grasped them immediately with her keen mind.

"Then we've only Patty and Dee to worry us," she said.

"And maybe Carol, if Patty has turned her loose. And Dee has a gun."

Agnes said, "Patty has one, too. He must have. He took it with him this morning when he went out to work on the apple trees."

Her words jolted me, almost like a blow. I almost blurted their effect to Agnes, but caught myself in time. I didn't want her worrying.

I said, "What time did Patty go into the orchard this morning?"

She hesitated, "I don't know exactly. But it was immediately after you and Manie and the others left for Winslow."

"And Carol stayed with you?"

"Yes, until just a little while ago, when I escaped."

I nodded, not liking what was in my mind. I said, "Look, you stay here. I think you'll be as safe as any place. Wait a half hour, then come back to the farm, but try to keep out of sight until you find me. Do you understand?"

"Yes, Johnny, but—"

I insisted, "Do as I say. I have to wind this damn mess up, and I don't want you either hurt or in the way."

"But can't I help, Johnny?"

"No."

She smiled, leaned forward and kissed me. "All right, Johnny."

I rose then and started back along the muddy footpath. Uppermost in my mind was not Agnes, then—not even her kiss. Something was terribly wrong. What bothered me was—if Carol had been with Agnes, and if Patty Sears was hacking at the cement in the trees since morning, who the hell tipped off the police and drove the blue coupe Dee and I had chased in from Winslow?

21

THERE WAS only one logical explanation. Someone else
had been rung in on the deal. Everyone I knew had been
accounted for every minute of the day and no mirage
had crashed me off the road. Then who had? Some friend
of Patty Sears?

I did a belly crawl most of the way when I came within
sight of the farm house. I came up behind the barn, flat-
tened myself against it. Patty's car was still there. Then,
peering around the corner, I froze.

Dee, apparently just getting over the accident, was
struggling up the driveway. She didn't look to her left
or right, but stared straight ahead trudging wearily and
with obvious disgust. She reached the porch, sighed
deeply, entered the house and slammed the door behind
her.

I slipped into the barn, mounted the stairs. Carol was
in her room, still securely bound. She writhed as she saw
me, as though she wanted to tell me something.

I grinned sourly at her and said, "Tough, kid."

Through a lull in the storm I heard a noise outside.
A car door slammed. Had reinforcements arrived—and
for whom? Were they police, or friends of Patty? I went
to the window and looked. Whoever had come had arrived in style. A giant black Cadillac was parked next

to the house. Luxurious, solid, with plenty of chrome, it glistened like a large opal in the rain.

I turned to Carol and asked, "Expecting company?"

She shook her hear tearfully. For the first time I noticed that she was finding it hard to breathe. Her face was red and she was making choking sounds. It could have been an act, but I didn't think so. I pulled the tape from her mouth.

She gulped for air convulsively, then stared at me in fright.

"Please, Johnny," she whispered. "I had to do it, try to believe me. I didn't want murder—and Patty Sears said he was going to kill your girl friend—that Agnes—unless I brought you back with me. He brought her here that evening."

"Sure," I said. "I'll bet he threatened to kill me too."

"He did! He did!" She started to cry. She rolled over on her side, away from me, so I couldn't see the lie in her eyes.

I pulled her back again. "And at the pool, Carol? That was for real?"

"I said I loved you. I meant it."

"You had one hell of a way of proving it."

"But Patty said—"

"Save it," I told her sharply. "Patty had a gun. Where is it now?"

She had no intention of answering me. Again she rolled over, shaking her head from side to side. She continued to cry. She had made her bid and lost.

I left her there and began my search. I attacked everything in the room. I wrecked her closet, dumped every drawer out, flipped the mattresses. I moved everything that could be moved, but found no weapon of any kind.

The hell with it.

164

SO LOVELY TO KILL

Without another word to Carol, I went down the stairs and out.

The Caddy still squatted next to the main house, sleek with rain. I could see no life in or about it. I said to hell with caution and dashed out to it and yanked open the door.

I found no identification either in the car or the glove compartment, and looked toward the farmhouse. Through a glossy windowpane I saw Dee. She was holding her little idiotic toy pistol, a .25, and she used it like a baton to give me instructions. She wanted me in.

I left the car, mounted the sagging porch. The door was already open—Dee was waiting for me. She held the pistol loosely.

She said frantically, "He's here."

"Who?"

"Manie. I don't know how he got here. He's here!"

Tears flodded her eyes. She waved the little gun in the direction of the living room. "He's in there."

"Is he hurt?"

"Yes."

"Bad?"

"I think so." She leaned against me and continued to cry. After a while she asked, "Carol? Where is she? Did she get the money?"

"No. It's not hidden in the trees."

She forgot that I wasn't supposed to be aware of the hiding place, and greeted the news with a juicy, descriptive phrase. Then she said, "Apple—what are we going to do?"

"We'll ask Manie."

She pulled herself together and looked at me wide-eyed. "I don't know if you can. He's hurt real bad. There's a first aid kit upstairs, but I don't know—"

165

SO LOVELY TO KILL

I said, "Get it," and watched her disappear up the staircase.

I went into the living room to look at Manie. He was on the sofa. He seemed dead. His powerful frame was motionless, his eyes half closed. His hands were folded across his front. He had caught one pretty. A large area of his white shirt was saturated with blood. Suddenly he moaned and his body jerked spasmodically with pain.

His .38 was on the coffee table next to him, and on the floor was an empty pillowcase. It was soaked with blood, but there was no money. He had done everything he had planned to do, except successfully rob the bank. At least his initiative rated some applause.

I went over to him, pulled up a chair and sat down. He heard the sound and his eyes focused on me. Through his agony his eyes narrowed and he gave me that too-friendly smile. "Hi, Apple. Glad to see you made it."

I didn't reply and removed his hands from the wound. It was bad. A bullet had caught him toward his left side, passed through his body and it was obvious that some of his vital organs were damaged. Staring at the ugly hole I knew that his death was simply a matter of time, unless he got to a doctor—and maybe that wouldn't save him.

I had no use for Manie Grass, but when a guy is dying you don't twist the blade. As gently as I could, I said, "You need help, Manie."

He shook his head. "Dee will fix me up. She'll do it good."

"She won't do that good. You need a doctor."

He thought about it and nodded. "All right—Albany. We'll drive to Albany. There—there's a doc there I know. He'll . . ."

I didn't argue with him, but he'd never last to Albany.

166

He needed aid immediately, so maybe it was wise just to forget it—sit there and watch him die.

He shifted his weight, winced, then smiled, apparently finding a more comfortable position. He was a tough claw and, for the record, had courage of a kind. He had been hurt, but he had asked to be and now he just lay there and took it.

"How did you get out of that mess?" I asked.

He put his hands over the wound again and laughed. He shouldn't have—the laughter choked off and he convulsed in pain.

"It happened so damned quick," he said. "At first I thought it was you—I thought you didn't fix the alarm."

"I fixed it."

"I know. There was a tip-off." Without mentioning Carol by name, and without any apparent malice toward her, he added: "I should have guessed. She'd been acting funny." He started to shift position, thought better of it, and settled back. "I'll—I'll have to tan her backside." He looked straight into my eyes. "She's okay, though? She's all right, huh?"

"She's fine."

"She don't mean nothing, you know. Just gets sort of uppity sometimes."

"Yeah, uppity," I said. "The hell with it. How did you get out?"

He tried another laugh, decided against it. "That was a riot," he said. "I took one of them bank executives out with me, a real stuffy bastard. I made him walk in front of me. The jerks! They shot anyway. They hit this guy in the leg and I got it in the belly. But they stopped shooting when they saw who I got with me." He paused, then went on. "I made him walk me right to his car and drive me out. I told 'em if I saw a roadblock or

167

anybody following, I'd shoot the louse. Nobody tried nothing—I guess they figured I was dying anyway."

"This executive? Did you kill him?"

He winced, and not from the pain. "Kill him? Why kill him? I dumped him about ten miles from town. Phone lines are down—be hours before he can get back to the cops."

He was quiet then, and his eyes were closed. He took several large gulps of air, and each exhalation was accompanied by a moan. I said nothing and watched him and, whatever I felt, I felt no pity at all.

Dee returned, still clutching her pistol. I tried to take it from her, but she shook her head, thrust it into her blouse. She opened the first aid kit and bent to administer to Manie.

A sound at the door caused me to turn. Patty Sears stood there, his grin ape-like, his gun as usual when he held it, pointed at me.

Dee saw him and gasped. "What are you doing here?"

Patty said, "Have the gentleman turn around."

Dee looked from one to the other of us, uncertain, baffled. "What does he mean, Apple?"

I shrugged.

Patty's grin tightened. His eyes narrowed. "I mean it, baby—have him turn around. You'll see what I mean."

Dee looked at me. He hand hovered in an unmistakable signal at the hem of her blouse, near the hidden .25. I think she meant to convey that if I could distract Patty enough, she could get at her gun before he could fire.

She said, "Maybe you'd better do as he says, honey."

I started to turn slowly, heard Dee suck in her breath quickly, then spun around fast, expecting to see her shooting at Patty. Instead, she was glaring at me with a fury that bordered on violence, her hand still clawing under her blouse. She spat an obscene word at me . . .

In the doorway Patty was doubled up with silent laughter, his gun no longer a factor.

I heard Manie groan a curse, then: "Shoot the bastard, Dee!"

He, too, meant me.

There was something here that all of them understood. I didn't—but I understood I had to get out fast. Dee's hand was just coming out of her blouse when I bolted.

My break was that Patty had no relish for using his gun, as long as there was someone else to do his shooting for him. I dashed for the door and spun left, toward the staircase. Patty ducked aside as, behind me, Dee's little gun cracked. In front of me plaster puffed into powder and the tiny bullet sank into the wall.

I streaked up the stairs, taking two and three steps at a time, as Dee's gun cracked again and again. I lost track of the shots—then I was out of range on the upper landing, and scrambling for the attic.

In the attic the first object to catch my eye was a large dressmaker's dummy. I grabbed it, heaved it at the gray square of a dormer window. It shattered the glass and took most of the frame with it. I dove for the opening, reached out and managed to hook my fingers on the gable above. I shoved out the window, got both hands on the gable, heaved upward and managed to scramble to the roof.

I barely made it before Dee and Patty burst into the attic below me. They seemed to have become at least temporary allies, but had been delayed by having to search the second floor for me. The crash of the breaking window had probably told them where I was. Clinging precariously to the wet, rotted shingles, I listened.

Dee said, "He must have gone out the window," and

169

their voices came more clearly.

Patty said, "There's something down there in the mud—"

Their voices receded again; they had gone down to investigate what I imagined must be the dressmaker's dummy.

I moved gingerly up an angle of the roof formed by the dormer gable. By digging my toes into the shingles and holding on to the top of the gable, I managed to work my way to the leeward side, slightly out of the wind. Below me the porch door slammed and once more I heard Dee's and Patty's voices. They discovered the dummy and Dee swore luridly, viciously. I inched to a spot on the roof from where I could see her. She was scanning the yard in every direction. Finally she glanced upward and I ducked.

The next half hour was agony. Dee and Patty circled the grounds, searching for me. Partly by luck, partly using my eyes and ears, I managed to stay out of their vision, dragging my numbed body around the storm-lashed roof.

Then I heard a voice calling my name thinly through the storm: "Johnny—Johnny—"

Agnes, approaching the house from the opposite direction from Dee and Patty, had spotted me. I had told her to wait a half-hour before coming to look for me—how long ago? How long had she been searching? I didn't know. I had lost all track of time.

I waved frantically at her to keep quiet, saw Dee and Patty run around a corner of the house to meet her. I scrambled to safety just in time. Peering over a gable, I saw Dee stride to Agnes, speak to her at gunpoint, then march her into the house. Patty went with her. Evidently they had given up the search for the moment.

SO LOVELY TO KILL

I don't know how much longer I stayed on the roof. The color of the day made it impossible to tell even the approximate hour. I listened and waited for some indication of Dee's next move, but all of them stayed indoors. I still didn't know what had turned Dee against me, and, try as I might, I could think of no explanation.

Finally I knew I had to move. The day had darkened— I guessed it was late afternoon. The storm showed no signs of abating, and the cold had all but rendered me helpless to move. In another few moments I *would* be helpless —and the only way down was the way I had come, through the broken window.

Painfully I inched my way to the gable over the broken window. For some time I had heard no sounds from the attic—nevertheless I paused again to listen. Nothing. Carefully, I lowered my legs over the end of the gable, hooked my arms over the peak. I felt the window sill under my feet, took a deep breath and lowered myself. My numbed arms began to slip—I felt myself falling, flailed desperately, caught the upper edge of the window frame with one hand just as my feet slid off the rain-soaked sill.

I fell—inside the attic. I felt the hard jar as my back hit the windowsill, then I was safe, lying gratefully on the floor of the attic, away from the wind and the rain.

I crawled away from the window, into a dry, dark corner. The relief of being out of the storm and cold was tremendous, as warmth gradually seeped back into my bones. I tried standing up and moving after a while, but even when I could trust my limbs, my teeth still chattered. I felt as close to pneumonia as the real Apple Renney had ever been.

Finally I eased the attic door open a crack and listened. The scuffing movements I heard all seemed to come from the first floor. I crept down to my room,

171

stripped and toweled—and at last discovered what had caused Dee's sudden rage when Patty had made me turn around, downstairs.

The faked birthmark—the apple—the symbol of my identity as the bank robber's friend—was gone from my hip, vanished without a trace! I swore as luridly as Dee herself had done. I cursed Matt and his hare-brained schemes—I cursed the tattoo artist who had sworn his work would last at least six weeks or more, and finally cursed myself for having been damned fool enough to have believed either one of them.

Then I was mad. I found some clothes—just a shirt and pants and shoes—and climbed into them. Swiftly I prowled the second floor rooms for a knife, a gun, a weapon of any kind, but found nothing. I paused at the head of the stairs. I had to go down, get into the kitchen— there I could find at least a knife.

The house was darkening rapidly. The electric lines were down. Perhaps in the dusk I might be able to slip unnoticed into the kitchen. The murmur of voices from below told me nothing, but seemed to come from the living room. I started down, slowly.

The only light on the first floor came from the living room. I paused in the shadows outside the open door, looked in.

Two kerosene lanterns, one on the table, another on the floor, cast just enough light to see. Manie was on the sofa and, apparently, he had not been moved since the last time I had seen him. Dee stood over him with what I thought was a whip in her hand. It wasn't, however. It was a thick length of insulated wire. As I watched, she lashed his body with it, again and again, and to say that it wouldn't do the same damage as a whip would be quibbling.

SO LOVELY TO KILL

Patty held Carol, who was struggling silently, desperately, to go to Manie's aid. Evidently her hatred for Manie did not extend to torture, but Patty handled her easily. Agnes huddled in a corner away from the light. Her face was expressionless.

I looked back at Manie. I doubted he felt Dee's savage ministrations—he seemed to be out cold. Fresh bandages girded his waist. The job looked professional, and I knew Agnes had done it. Maybe she had bargained for her life by keeping Manie alive until he could tell them where he had hidden the money.

The guns, Manie's, Patty's and Dee's pistols, were on the coffee table and that indicated that a truce had been agreed on. This was evidently a time for cooperation among the vultures—their aims were the same and, until they got what they wanted, they were useful to each other.

I knew this situation could not last. Patty and Carol had planned too carefully and Dee was not part of their plans. They would not share the bazooka money with her, and her position was even more positive. She had already killed in her quest for the money. She would do it again.

I heard Dee say, "Wake him up again," and Agnes moved obediently away from the corner and went to the first aid kit. She was watched keenly, every eye upon her every move.

I thought of a weapon again, and for a moment considered making a try for one of the guns on the coffee table. But I would never make it in my present condition —the kitchen was my only chance. I slipped unobtrusively away, feeling my way along the darkened passage. I had another thought—Manie's whiskey bottle. I had seen it on the kitchen table this morning. It was probably still somewhere in the kitchen tonight. As much as a weapon, I could use a drink at this point.

173

SO LOVELY TO KILL

I found the whiskey first and took a healthy swig. The liquid raced to the bottom of my stomach, turned around and started back out of me. My abused system did not take kindly to it—I sat down on the floor, fighting nausea, and gradually won. The warmth of the liquor dissipated itself through my ravaged body, and I felt better. I stood up, took a slower drink, then another, and now it really took hold.

I rummaged in several draweres for a knife, and finally came up with a cutter almost heavy enough to be used as a machete, and still capable of being concealed, at least temporarily, under the waistband of my trousers. Thus armed, I began to make my way back toward the living room.

Agnes was back in her corner, but she was watched closely by Patty. In fact, Patty's eyes were darts, now on Dee, next on Carol, next on Agnes. He had picked up his gun. Carol had become her hard-rock self again, saying nothing, hating all of them with her eyes.

I don't know what Agnes had done to Manie, but she had succeeded in bringing him back from unconsciousness and, strangely, he seemed to be gaining in strength. It was probably a final surge of the will to live that, sometimes, immediately precedes death. He had pushed himself up on his elbows, though his eyes were glassy and he was a million miles away.

"The money, Manie," Dee urged. "Where's the money?" She nudged him. "Tell me, honey. Tell me where the money is?"

She put the thought in his head, as she probably had been doing all afternoon and evening, and waited for a positive reply. She didn't get one. But he moved, pushing himself up farther, and the weight of his big legs forced Dee back slightly as he swung them to the floor.

174

SO LOVELY TO KILL

She brightened, wickedly. "That's it, Manie. Get your money. Don't tell me where it is. Don't tell anyone. Get it. Do you hear, Manie? Get your money!"

Again he nodded and mumbled something thickly and rose like a zombie. Dee supported him and, for a reason that was even beyond him, he didn't approve. His arm swept around and Dee was pushed away. I couldn't see her face, but I knew she was elated.

Then Manie muttered the one word that made sense. "My money—"

Dee was so excited she shook. Patty grabbed the lantern from the floor and Dee thrust it into Manie's hand. "There, so you can see. There! Go ahead now. Get your money!"

He started for the door. I don't know how, but he did. Slowly, stolidly, staggering, he thumped forward.

Patty grabbed the other lantern, gave it to Agnes, motioned her to go ahead of him. They all went out ahead of Manie, except Dee. When the others had reached the door, she spun around quickly, remembering the other guns.

It was then I acted. I stumbled forward in a rush, but mine were elephant legs, much too heavy for my body. I had a distance of only fifteen feet to travel, yet it seemed like a thousand. Dee saw me and gasped. I dove.

The room was suddenly dark—the others had taken all illumination with them. Dee and I hit the coffee table together. I struck once in her direction with my butcher knife, missed and felt the weapon jump from my hand. Then I was groping frantically for one of the guns, found it just as gun flame blossomed two feet from my face. The explosion was lost in a clap of thunder.

Dee had the other gun—Manie's. I had wound up with her tiny .25. She had fired once, perhaps by accident, perhaps hoping to hit me—now we both waited. I hadn't the faintest idea of where she was.

A minute passed before she spoke, her voice a little frantic. "I'll make a deal with you, Fury. There's one bullet in that gun of mine, if you found it—I've got five more bullets, and mine are bigger. Will you listen?"

I said nothing, afraid that she would shoot at my voice, thinking that she was probably right about the gun I held. When you have one bullet in a .25, you don't take chances on missing.

She spoke again. "I've got to go out there—Manie's taking them to the money. Think of it, Fury—a half million for us to split, if you help me get rid of the others. I don't trust Patty any more than I trust you. And I—we loved once—remember?"

She stopped, listening, then laughed suddenly, a little desperately. "All right—it's got to be a deal. I'm going out now—" She moved to the door and out. I didn't try to stop her.

I stood up and found myself sweating coldly, clammily. I broke open the little gun in the darkness, and found she had been right—there was just one bullet left in the magazine. It was nothing to tackle a desperate bunch with and I thought that for the moment at least, Dee had herself a deal. I shoved the gun in my pocket and went out.

Manie and the others hadn't gotten far. They made a small, lantern-lit huddle at the rear of the house, and Manie's shoulders hunched so low his hands seemed almost to touch the ground. Patty had taken the lantern away from him and he was no longer muttering. He was breathing heavily and staring fixedly at nothing. Manie Grass was far beyond the point of pain. He didn't even know enough to fight for his life. Instinct had taken over.

SO LOVELY TO KILL

Patty snarled, "Damn it, Manie, where the hell did you put that money?"

I felt something move beside me in the darkness. It was Dee. She gripped Manie's big revolver, but didn't point it at me. She glanced at me, but mostly her eyes were fixed on the group ahead.

She said very softly, "I meant that about a deal, Fury. I need help and I don't care where I get it. I could have killed you a second ago—"

I nodded. "It's a deal—for now."

We moved up together. Patty jumped and his gun came around when he saw us, but Dee's weapon covered him. "Forget it," she said tightly. "I asked him to work with us. I figured I could use him on my side."

"How the devil—" Patty started to say.

Dee smiled at him and her gun was steady. "He's tough," she said. "He just doesn't want to die."

Neither did Patty. He subsided, glowering.

This time Manie interrupted. His breath wheezing, his lungs straining for air, he gasped, "Mildred—"

Just that one word, that name, and it was enough. We understood. Dee and Carol and I knew that Manie had obliged, finally, now that it could never do him any good. We glanced at one another briefly and, I guess, I should have figured it out long ago. A hiding place as bizarre as an apple tree wouldn't have appealed to Manie. He would have been direct about it and impulsive enough to plant his loot in the first good spot that came to mind. One that wouldn't be disturbed easily. Apple trees were for the living. He doctored them because he liked them and wanted them to survive.

He said, "Mildred—" once more before he died. Then he stiffened, balanced precariously between here and there, and crashed to the ground. He fell as a tree falls.

177

His face sank into the mud and he did not move.

Carol spun around quickly, not wanting to see. The others were unconcerned.

Patty said, "Who's Mildred?"

Dee's eyes were very bright. I think she might have started shooting us all right there if Carol hadn't spoken.

"Mildred Causby is buried down by the river," Carol said. "The money must be hidden in her grave."

By then the moment was broken. Patty's hand was in his pocket, probably gripping his gun; my fist had closed over Dee's little .25, with the one futile bullet in it—still effective enough at this range.

Dee shrugged. "Let's get some shovels," she said. "It'll take all of us to dig."

I wondered if the others thought she meant what I thought she did.

22

WE MARCHED in file, a miserable, bedraggled safari, and again confronted the wailing forest. I led—it was Patty's suggestion—and carried a lantern in one hand and a spade in the other. Agnes, walking just behind me, half-carried, half-dragged another shovel.

I didn't know if she had grasped the significance of our trip. She seemed too stunned by the succession of events which had started out, for her, with a kidnapping, and now threatened to end with wholesale execution. I wondered if she fully realized that we were going to the graves for another reason besides the money. I was sure that Dee, at least, had thought of our digging in terms of new graves. I wasn't sure of Patty—he might or might not be a killer. Occasionally, when I glanced back, I saw that Patty and Dee brought up the rear of the procession almost side by side. Neither could afford to let the other lag behind.

We reached the grave, and my skin contracted until my flesh was hard with little bumps. The others came up and we formed a circle, and still there was no conversation. We stared at the grave, at each other. Meditation hour? Sure. Hour of victory—for whom? Hour of end—again for whom? Thunder clapped with enough power to shake the earth. Our alliances were weak and fragile, based on selfishness, distrust and fear. Dee's and mine. Dee's and Patty's. Carol's and Patty's. Agnes alone had made no deals with anybody—she had nothing on her side except my determination to help her. And what would I actually do against Dee's gun—against Patty's?

We finally got to work, digging in shifts based on mutual suspicion. First Carol and I, leaving Dee and Patty free to watch each other. Then Agnes relieved Carol, and finally Patty relieved me.

The digging was tough, much tougher, I thought, than it should have been, if Manie had really buried anything here as recently as the bazooka robbery. Still, the others seemed to notice nothing amiss, and the temporary truce under which we labored gave me a chance to think. There was one large question still unanswered—who had driven the blue coupe Dee and I had followed this morning from Winslow?

My brain was sluggish, refused to answer. The storm continued to lash down on us, and the rain turned our efforts to quagmire. Dee, Carol and I sat slightly, distrustfully apart, watching each other, watching Patty and Agnes. Once I thought Carol tried to signal to me, tried to tell me something, but when I looked again, her eyes had gone dead.

I remember thinking that of the five of us, only Dee seemed to have the drive and vitality to remain fully alert. Her eyes flicked constantly from one to the other of us— she trusted no one, expected no trust. And she was right, of course.

Finally it was Carol's and my turn again—Dee refused to do any of the manual labor, and it was easier not to argue. Besides, as Manie's widow, perhaps she had an unwritten right to direct operations. Carol and I took the shovels from Agnes and Patty, and sloshed into

180

the excavation. The water was well above our ankles and, since we couldn't see the bottom, footing was precarious. Carol lurched once against me, grabbed my arm to keep from falling, and all at once I felt her pressing herself hard against my side.

"Johnny," she whispered, the sound barely audible, the wind carrying her breath away almost immediately. "Johnny—I saw Patty give Agnes his gun. Agnes has Patty's gun—"

I shoved her roughly away—then her words penetrated. I started to say, "What the hell—" glanced at her and realized she had dug her shovel hard into the dirt, was trying to dig furiously. Mostly to give myself time to think, I dug down, too—and my shovel hit a hard tangle of roots, heavy roots, roots that couldn't possibly have grown here since Manie had hidden his half-million.

And all at once everything hit me. The money wasn't here—couldn't be here. Patty and Agnes must have run into the same roots, must have realized what I had just realized. Yet they had said nothing—and just now Carol had told me Patty had given Agnes his gun while they were down here in the hole, digging side by side! Suddenly, in an all-around flash, I saw the whole picture. Carol hadn't sent for Patty—Agnes had *brought* Patty, while pretending to be kidnapped. Agnes and Patty were in this together . . . I didn't have time to analyze it further.

Carol's elbow hit mine, and when I glanced at her, there was a strange, half-pleading, half-questioning look in her eyes. I nodded at her, tried to grin and swore.

I whispered, "What a goddamned fool I am!" and through the wind and the rain she must have understood. Her face was muddy, tired, and the storm had lashed her hair stringily all around it. But suddenly it wore an expression of radiant confidence and gladness.

181

She started to say something, when Dee's voice came stridently from above us.

"What are you two talking about?" Dee wanted to know.

Carol had the answer—I realized later that she had thought all this out while we had been resting on the rim of the hole. She glanced at me, smiled faintly, whispered, "All together now, Johnny," and dug her shovel into the dirt.

Aloud, she said, "I think I've hit paydirt!"

Patty, Dee and Agnes strained forward and Carol and I dug into the earth and water. I just followed the leader. Carol brought up her shovel and her spadeful of mud caught Agnes hard in the face. I was a second slower, but managed to catch on in time to give Dee a mudpack. In the same movement I brought my shovel around and tried to cut Patty's head off at the neck—there was a fierce hope and joy of combat in me at this moment.

Patty rolled with my swing, but the shovel caught him on the side of the head hard enough to knock him down. Then Carol and I were out of the hole and I had tangled with Dee.

She fought with all her unwomanly strength, but without the weapons she had used against me on the night of my arrival, she was no match. I wrested the gun from her and left her, still blinded with mud, and turned to meet Patty's rush. He came at me staggering, his head bleeding from the blow of my shovel—I think it was berserk fear rather than courage that drove him. I struck down his groping arms, brought the gun barrel down on his head and he sank, groaning, to his knees.

Beside me a gun went off, twice. I saw Carol tangling with Agnes, and realized with a gust of relief that she was smart enough to concentrate on hanging on to Agnes' gun wrist, spoiling her aim. I stepped over, kicked the gun out of Agnes' hand, pulled Carol clear . . .

And it was all over.

I guess, if there had been anyone to see, we would have presented a fantastic picture—a battlefield in miniature. The five of us wet, muddy, and each to his own degree battered and bleeding. And wearily, hopelessly hating.

Dee was writhing on the ground in an ecstasy of anger and frustration, moaning, "Kill him—shoot the bastard, Patty . . . kill them both . . ." and in spite of everything I had to laugh. A moment ago she had been running the show—now she still didn't quite realize what had happened.

I went over and picked up Patty's gun, the gun I had kicked out of Anges' hand. I showed both guns to Dee, to all of them. I said, "The show's over. The money isn't here. Dee—we were both taken in by a sweet little double-cross. Agnes and Patty, here—the reason he didn't shoot me just then was that he'd given his gun to Agnes, hoping to take you off guard. Me, too." And they would have succeeded if it hadn't been for Carol, I thought.

I watched it sink in, first with Dee, then with Agnes. Neither was pretty. I felt Carol at my side and told them, "All right, on your feet. Line up and let's get back—we've got a long walk."

We started back, a sad procession, Agnes, Dee and Patty blazing the way through the gale-tossed woods, Carol and I bringing up the rear. I remember thinking that actually I understood very little of it yet—that there were a number of threads to tie in—but I knew two important things. One, I had the guns and control, and it seemed for the first time in an eternity as though I were going to be around for a little while longer. Two, Carol was clinging to my arm, staggering at my side and, though

SO LOVELY TO KILL

I doubt that either of us felt very emotional, her touch was good. It belonged.

I was tired, but like a broken record Agnes and the events of the past few days kept turning over in my mind. Just when had she gotten on the half-million-dollar bandwagon—when had she grown greedy? It could have been that night in my apartment, when she had come to help me pack and I had repulsed her, but actually I thought it would have been earlier. She would have been like that always. You don't go on a kick like this on a moment's notice, and I was glad now I had never gone overboard for her. It hadn't been only her hands that repelled me, but Agnes herself. It wasn't only that she had chosen a morbid life's work—she was a morbid, mad, dangerous woman.

It was she, not some outsider, who had driven Patty's blue coupe this morning. It was not she who had been the captive in Carol's room last night—but Carol herself. And Carol had been telling the truth right along . . .

I felt stupid, used up and lousy. As far back as our last date in New York, Agnes had indicated her interest in more money than the thirty-grand reward I was to get for getting the goods on Manie Grass. I remembered she had asked me about the possible profits from a successful bank robbery. And when I had shut her up in no uncertain terms, she had sulked.

That brought me to the question of where Manie had actually hidden the bazooka money. My mind pushed at the problem tiredly, not really caring—and, as sometimes happens, I had the answer instantly. Probably I would have had it earlier, if all our minds had not been occupied with the conviction that Manie had been talking

184

of Mildred's grave. Where else was there something of Mildred's—probably a damned sight more substantial than anything left in the grave?

I knew now, with almost total certainty—but the knowledge gave me no elation.

It was the longest walk I have even taken. We didn't speak much, any of us. Carol and I clung together, but our main concern was to help each other over the rough spots of the trail and storm, not in an exchange of amenities. And though we felt—it was not emotion.

We reached the farm at last, and almost simultaneously heard it—the faint, distant wail of a siren. Satisfaction stirred in me sluggishly—the police were on their way. It would have taken them all day to get through to Matt Nugent through the storm, but once they had, he had told them where to come.

I collapsed on the porch of the farmhouse and motioned my little gang of killers to sit down, too. There was no point, now, in going indoors, and in my present condition I didn't want to trust them in the intricacies of doorways.

Besides, I had something to tell them.

"Listen," I said. "Over there, under a busted dormer window, is a dressmaker's dummy. If my hunch is right, it's probably the most expensive one in the world. It ought to be worth about a half a million in unspendable currency."

I wanted to see their faces. I needed something to keep me awake until the cops came.

Dee was the first to get it. She bolted upright. She gasped, "Mildred!"

It almost killed her. She had been living with it all the time, day in and day out. There was Mildred in the mud, the dressmaker's mannikin, the Mildred I had used to

185

knock out the dormer window, the Mildred Manie had muttered of before he died, and we had mistaken it for the grave. This was the size and shape of Mildred—something Manie would probably have remembered much beyond her rotting bones.

Dee was itching to get it, even though she knew she would never keep a single cent of it—Manie's half-million. She just wanted to feel it, to see it and to think that, at least for an instant, it had been a part of her. More slowly, I thought, the others caught her fever—all except Carol, who remained at my side.

I kept the gun on them all, feeling a tiny amount of strength seep back into my bones. The police were coming, and everything was well in hand. I just hoped to hell they would hurry. Now that my select group of cut-throats sensed the nearness of their dreams, they were growing restive again.

I held them. God knows how. But presently we heard motors and the patrol cars came up the driveway. There was a minor crash, and I guessed that one of the cars had nudged the black Cadillac. They hadn't been able to see it, coming quietly, with their headlights off.

I heard Matt's voice calling guardedly, "Johnny!"

"It's all right," I shouted. "For God's sake, Matt—the lights! Put on the lights!"

As I said it, Dee screamed and I spun around. She had broken from the group and reached the mannikin and, as the police floodlights and headlights bathed the area, I saw an eerie sight. The air was filled with money, like a migration of birds, birds of ten, twenty and one hundred dollar denominations. They fluttered crazily, zigzagged nervously in the gale, as though elated to be released from their damp dungeon. They skirled faster than autumn leaves.

186

SO LOVELY TO KILL

Then came the screams and, as well as I knew her it was hard for me to believe that these eldritch sounds emanated from Dee Grass. As crazily as the money flew, she flew after it. Her arms flailed in the storm-swept glare, her fingers clutching like a mad zoo keeper's trying to hinder the escape of his favorite flock. I saw her running and sensed action around me as Matt roared up and helped me retain the loose money in the mannikin.

The other cops were just as efficient. One grabbed Patty and another Carol, almost as if they had rehearsed it, as they probably had.

I shouted at Matt, though his ear was only a few inches away, "Not Carol—she's clean. Get Agnes, dammit!" And I was shaking my fist at Agnes.

Matt stood up and ran and his fat legs got him to her with amazing speed. Agnes, naturally, was still innocent in Matt's eyes, and she had been using it as her last chance. She tried to walk casually away. But where could she walk to? She could never hide. The world had become too small for her. She didn't really resist Matt's hand on her arm.

One cop was after Dee but he didn't catch her because she wasn't running away. She darted in zigzags, clutching and screaming and even as she vanished into the orchard I knew what she could never know—that she hadn't retained a single dollar bill.

Then there were no screams. They stopped abruptly, the last one being cut off in the middle and I knew that something had happened. Maybe it had something to do with the crash of a tree, maybe not. I didn't know. I didn't care. I didn't want any part of it. Not now. It was too late to want to be a part of Dee or Agnes or anything associated with the Causby farm.

Except Carol. She was holding me and crying softly.

187

SO LOVELY TO KILL

I heard a lobster shout from the orchard, "Here's Manie's wife—she got herself run over by a tree."

I heard Matt respond. "Is she hurt?"

The cop replied, "Hell, she's dead."

In the orchard. It would be an apple tree and it seemed appropriate.

A cop laid a tarpaulin over the mannikin and then he sat on it, waiting for further instructions.

Carol helped me to my feet and led me to a patrol car. I dragged myself into the back seat and she fell in next to me. A cop tossed a blanket over us, then got in the front seat, behind the wheel.

Matt came over but he said nothing to me. He just looked.

The cop in front said, "What'll I do?"

Matt was no longer the jolly lobster. He said gruffly, "What the hell do you think? Take him to a hospital!"

The car backed up, then rolled down to the black macadam road. Carol clung to me and I clung to her, as though we were one. Her warmth flowed into me, deliciously, as we inched our way through the mad naked summer night.

THE END

188